the last free cat

jon blake

albert whitman & company
chicago, illinois

In loving memory of Floozie (1995–2008)

Library of Congress Cataloging-in-Publication Data

Blake, Jon.
The last free cat / by Jon Blake.
p. cm.
Summary: In a future world where only the wealthy can afford to own cats, and
only felines bred by the Viafara corporation are legal, Jade finds a beautiful stray cat
and risks everything to keep it, aided by her friend Kris.
ISBN 978-0-8075-4364-1 (hardcover)
[1. Cats—Fiction. 2. Government, Resistance to—Fiction. 3. Social classes—
Fiction.
4. Criminals—Fiction. 5. Science fiction.] I. Title.
PZ7.B554Las 2012
[Fic]—dc23
2011035049

First published in Great Britain in 2008 by Hodder Children's Books.
Text copyright © Jon Blake 2008.
Published in 2012 by Albert Whitman & Company.

For more information about Albert Whitman & Company,
visit our web site at www.albertwhitman.com.

Chapter One

I kept one eye on Feela and one on the trap door. Down below I could make out the gruff voice of the Pets Inspector and Mum's faltering replies. Mum wasn't used to breaking the law. I felt guilty for putting her in this situation.

Muffled thuds. They were coming up the stairs. Mum's voice was getting louder as her anxiety grew. I reached to check the lock on the door and knocked over a bottle. Feela's eyes opened.

"Ssh!" I said stupidly. Feela stretched out her front feet for a big, bug-eyed yawn.

"What's up there?" I heard.

"Just the attic," replied Mum.

Feela stood up, stretched into a quivery arch, and padded to the edge of the bed. Quickly I reached over and tickled her chin. For the moment, she stayed put.

"I'm sorry to put you to this trouble," said the Pets Inspector.

"I'm sorry too," replied Mum.

"The cat was seen in your garden," said the Pets Inspector.

"So you said," replied Mum.

Feela's ear was cocked. She was recognizing Mum's voice. Suddenly she jumped. To my horror, she went straight over to the trap door and let out a tiny pink-mouthed cry.

Dead silence. The whole of my life hung in the balance. If the inspector came through that trap door, I wouldn't be seeing Mum for another five years. And I wouldn't be seeing Feela ever.

The voices rose again, this time farther away. Thank God. They were downstairs. Feela's cry hadn't carried.

The front door closed. He'd gone. Until now, I hadn't really felt afraid—just focused, like a racing driver at full speed. But as the relief came over me, my hands started to tremble uncontrollably. I scrabbled at the trap door, pulled it open, and found myself looking down at Mum's face, flushed pink and ten years older than before.

"*Never again,*" she declared. "*Never, never again.*"

"He's gone now," I consoled her.

"Until the next time," Mum replied.

"There won't be a next time," I countered.

"Of course there'll be a next time!" snapped Mum. "We can't keep that cat hidden forever!"

As if in reply, Feela jumped down onto Mum's shoulder, then used her like a climbing frame to get to the floor. I lowered the ladder and followed. Mum dropped into a chair, one hand to her head, fighting for breath.

"You see what this has done to me?" she gasped.

I squatted down next to Mum and took her hand. She'd had a weak heart for a few years now, and it wasn't getting any better. There were drugs which could cure it, but none that we could afford.

Mum noticed my hand was trembling. "You're becoming like me," she said, "a nervous wreck."

So what? I thought. Everyone in this horrible neighborhood had nervous problems. It was inevitable, like getting older. But at least with Feela, I had something worth living for.

I replayed in my mind the night we found her. Of course, we had seen cats before, but only onscreen, or in the wide windows of the houses on the mount. To find one, real and alive, in our moonlit garden, was breathtaking. We watched, transfixed, as it tested the scents of the grass, offered its chin to a small branch, then began to scrape a hole in the earth. Everything about it was so focused, so sure, so lithe in movement. The smallest noise, and its head was up, its ears swiveling like radar screens, its almond eyes watching. I loved the sweep of its tail, as bushy as a squirrel's, and the close gloss of its black, ginger, and white coat. From the little smile that played on Mum's lips, I could tell she felt the same.

"Where do you think it came from?" I whispered in a religious hush.

"It should say on the—"

Mum's sentence never ended. She had noticed something very wrong about the cat. It had no collar.

Chapter Two

When Great-Grandma was alive, she told me stories of a time when almost everyone had a cat. Incredible as it may seem, you could answer an ad in a pet-shop window, knock on someone's door, then go home with a kitten. Just like that, and not pay a cent! What a world that must have been!

But that was before the flu scare. HN51, the new and deadly strain of cat flu, which was passed to a human in Surinam and without quick action would have spread around the world like wildfire. After HN51, there was a worldwide cull of infected cats and ownership of cats became strictly monitored. All cats had to be registered, and over a period of time two big companies, Viafara and Chen, took over the whole business—breeding, vaccinating, and putting them on the market.

There weren't enough cats to go around. So the price went higher and higher, till only the very rich could afford them.

There was one girl in our school who had a cat. At least, she *said* she had a cat. But when we asked her if it was a Viafara or a Chen, she didn't seem to know. I think she was just trying to make herself sound big. Anyway, it all rebounded back on her, because her house got burgled so many times her family had to leave the area.

It wasn't surprising, really. Every time you turned on the screen there was another advert showing some beautiful cat, strolling around the pool in some fantastic mansion. Then you'd see the price. Two million euros, some of them! Is it any wonder cat kidnapping became such a common crime? Mind you, they had that under control now. It was pretty much impossible to get into the private neighborhoods unless you had a minicopter, and they cost almost as much as a cat.

The new collars had also put off the cat kidnappers. They all had tracking devices built in. For a while you could jam the Chen ones, but then Viafara bought out Chen and put the same processors in them, and made them pretty much foolproof. And since it was impossible to get the collar off without lopping the cat's head off, the chances of a kidnapper getting caught were roughly a hundred percent.

But our cat, as I've said, had no collar. That was the exciting—and frightening—thing about it.

"It's seen us," I said. The cat was staring steadily in our direction, caught between fear and curiosity. Then, unbelievably, it started to move towards us. Mum began to panic.

"Don't touch it!" she warned.

"Why not?"

"It might attack."

The cat didn't look like it was about to attack. But then, maybe that was the way they worked. Maybe they jumped suddenly, without warning. The fact was, we knew practically nothing about them, other than what Great-Grandma had told us.

"We'd better go in," said Mum.

Neither of us moved. Mum was as fascinated as I was. Everything about this creature cast a spell, and when it stood no more than a meter away, opened its needle-toothed mouth, and cried, we knew we couldn't ignore it.

"Maybe it's hungry," I said.

"Fetch some sardines," said Mum.

7

I was right about the cat being hungry. As soon as the sardines were on the ground, it checked around, then set about its meal with total abandon. Even when the last trace was gone, it kept on licking. Then it looked back up at us with a new and powerful interest.

"Let's let it in," I suggested, more in hope than expectation. Mum was horrified.

"It's a criminal offense!" she said.

"But it's lost!"

"Jade, it's an unregistered cat."

"But look at its face, Mum."

"It could be diseased!"

"It doesn't look diseased."

"Looks can be deceptive."

Mum said this with great weight, and a nodding of the head. When she spoke like this, out of grim experience, you didn't doubt her. But the pull of the cat was just as strong.

"If we took her in tonight, Mum—"

"Jade, no."

"Just tonight, Mum! Then ring the authorities in the morning!"

"Are *you* going to ring the authorities?"

"Yeah!"

Mum viewed me doubtfully.

"On my mother's life, Mum!" I blurted, not realizing what I was saying.

"Exactly," said Mum. "It *will* be on your mother's life."

"Please, Mum," I pleaded. "Just to have it in the house, for a few hours; just so we could say we had a cat once in our lives."

Mum smiled at my dramatic little speech. I sensed a weakness and pressed home the advantage with a lost-lamb look I had practiced all my childhood.

"On your head be it," she said, but as we've already established, both our heads were on the block from that moment.

Chapter Three

There was no way she'd let me touch her at first. Trust had to be built up slowly and painfully. I talked to her softly, offered her little treats, and took care not to make any sudden or threatening movements. Then, when Mum had gone to bed, I laid a trail of tuna flakes on the kitchen floor, got down flat to the ground, and arranged the last few morsels along my arm and on my back.

Time passed, maybe half an hour, then at last she crept out from her hidey-hole and began to take the bait. I hardly dared breathe as she drew up alongside me, still with that quivery watchfulness, but growing more confident all the time. And then, in one sacred moment, she snaffled the tuna from my arm, and I felt just a tickle of contact.

Hardly daring to breathe, I silently urged her on. She laid one testing paw upon my elbow, craned her neck, and took the next treat.

Two paws next, and a snaffle from my back—but that was as far as she could reach.

Stalemate.

I closed my eyes, desperately tired, and resigned myself to trying again in the morning. But I would not have to wait that long. Again she tested my arm with her paws, then, without warning, sprang softly onto my back. I lay still and steady, in quiet satisfaction, as she went about her business, nibbling the last of the tuna. Then, when she'd had her fill, I laid another trail and did exactly the same thing again. This time, lying beneath her gentle weight, I fell fast asleep. I was still there next morning when Mum came down; so was my little cat.

"Look at you!" she said, with a broad smile. Once she had smiled and laughed a lot, but it didn't happen often now.

"I want to keep her, Mum," I said. The words had escaped before I'd even thought about what I was saying.

"Jade, no," said Mum.

"But Mum," I protested, "what if they kill her?"

"They're not going to kill her," replied Mum, then gave a nervous little laugh, betraying the fact that she wasn't so sure.

"They *will* kill her," I replied, much more sure of myself.

"I'll ring them when I come back from Afshan's," asserted Mum.

Mum never did ring the authorities. By that evening I'd trained the cat to lie on my lap, and after tea she climbed onto Mum's, stretched her paw across like a baby, and closed her eyes. Mum absentmindedly stroked her head, and for the first time, the cat let out a purr.

"I think we should call her Feela," said Mum.

"Why?" I asked.

"It's a nice name," said Mum.

"OK," I replied.

Mum carried on stroking, saying nothing. Then, out of the blue, she said, "It's wrong, you know."

"What?" I asked.

"That we can't have things like this," said Mum.

It half frightened me to hear Mum say these words, but it thrilled me too. By and large, she was a woman who accepted her lot, who avoided argument at any cost, but there was a part of her which still had some fight in it, which sided with the underdog, which never fully accepted the way things were.

"Mum," I said, "I won't let her out. No one'll see her."

"You can't be sure of that," said Mum.

"I can, Mum!" I protested. "I can!"

Mum studied my pleading expression, as if hoping to be convinced.

"Let's keep her, Mum," I said softly.

Mum looked back at Feela, so beautiful, so composed, so very much at home. She sighed deeply.

"Looks like she's made up our minds for us," she said.

Chapter Four

For the next three weeks Feela was my life. I studied everything about her and, bit by bit, built a relationship with her. I couldn't believe how much she slept! All day sometimes, with just a break for a meal or to do a toilet in the box of earth we prepared for her. Yet she could come awake in an instant, be totally alert, and five seconds later be on a mad dash about the house. She did one of these mad dashes once every few days, and they really alarmed me. Her ears would go back, she'd skid around corners, then end up wrapped around a table leg with her back legs cycling furiously. There seemed no reason for it, unless it was the memory of some scary experience. Either way, I kept my distance while she was like that. At other times, though, she was as soft as a toy, chinning the edge of my finger till I stroked her, or climbing silently on to my lap. I'd never felt such a peaceful feeling as I did at these times. A rich, warm purr would stir inside her, building higher and higher to a sonorous *preep*. And I would glow with the wonder of having a living animal in our house, sharing our lives.

Just as I was studying Feela, Feela was studying me. She got to know all my habits—when I ate, when I got up, even when I went to the toilet. Soon she became a part of those habits. I'd wake up to a rough tongue licking my face, and eat with two serene eyes staring up expectantly. When I went upstairs, she'd speed ahead of me, check to see I was following, then lead me up the steps into my bedroom. We'd race each other to the bed. She'd flop down beside me so I could get my hand around her and whisk the warm, silky tufts of her belly. It all seemed such an unashamed luxury.

In all this time we kept the blinds in our front window closed. There were no front gardens on Ferry Street and precious little privacy. When we lived on the marina no one used to sit on our front window-sill, and they certainly didn't stare straight into our living room. But people were different here. They sat out on the street, shouted up and down it, had full-blast fights on it, and didn't seem to care what anyone thought, least of all us.

We were outsiders and probably always would be. Not because we were stuck up, because we weren't, but because we'd lived somewhere different, somewhere where people didn't shout or ride their bikes through the red lights. And, let's face it, we'd never have moved to Ferry Street if Dad hadn't died and there hadn't been that problem with the life insurance that I never understood.

At least we had some privacy out the back—high fences on all sides and pyracantha bushes with thorns like nails. In fact it took us quite a while to figure out how Feela had got in—a hole in the fence behind the shed, which Mum fixed with a tomato box. There was no danger now of her leaving the garden and getting lost. But since there were about fifty gardens adjoining each other on our block, where she came from remained a mystery.

Then, of course, there was school. It was impossible to keep your privacy there. Someone always wanted to know what was in your lunch box, or where your mum worked, or what you'd been doing with x over at y on the nth of z.

By and large, though, I steered clear of serious trouble. I wasn't part of any gang, and even though some people gave me a hard time and called me Marina because of where I used to live, I just wasn't the type that got picked on, not *really* picked on, like the ones that committed suicide. Maybe I just came across as a boring person who had no secrets worth knowing.

There was one person, however, who found me endlessly fascinating. Kris Delaney. Kris was the bane of my life. It was the entire aim of his existence to test me. I don't know why I interested him so much. It certainly bugged him that I wasn't born in the neighborhood and had lived in a greenhome and, OK, we'd had a boat, if only a small one. But Kris was different, too. You'd see him with the other lads, kicking a ball about, but you'd see him on his own just as much. There was always a distance between him and his mates. Some people said his parents were gypsies, and I believed it. There was something about that bony face, that mop of corkscrews and, most of all, those soulful brown eyes. He might have been beautiful if he didn't have that big loose mouth with its tombstone teeth. Seeing him looking out over the docklands, you might think he was composing poetry or something. But as far as I knew, he never did. Most of the time he just swore and made snarky remarks, like all the other boys.

I might have kept my secret forever if it weren't for Kris.

It started as an ordinary enough day, except that I tried to pick up Feela just before I left for school. I didn't often do this because it was one thing she wouldn't tolerate, but I lived in hope that one day she'd get used to it and let me hold her like a baby. No such luck this time. She hissed into my face (her breath always smelled of haddock, no matter what we'd fed her), struggled, and jumped free.

Ah well, I said to myself. Better luck next time. I thought no more of it, till Kris sought me out in the playground.

It started as the usual type of conversation. Kris told me how beautiful I was looking, which he always said, without giving any clue whether he meant it, was joking, or just looking for a reaction. I tried to ignore him as usual, but his gaze had become strangely fixed on my right shoulder. I turned away, but he came with me, peering closer and closer, till suddenly he snatched forward and plucked something from my sweater.

"Don't do that!" I barked.

Kris examined what looked like a piece of fine orange fluff. "That's cat hair," he said.

I died. "No it isn't!" I snapped.

Kris nodded. "Yes it is," he said. He peered again at my shoulder. "There's even flea eggs," he added.

"There is not!" I barked, covering the shoulder with my hand.

"Unless it's dandruff," said Kris.

"I do not have dandruff!" I cried.

"Just as I thought then," said Kris. "Flea eggs."

I made no reply. Was he bluffing me? I hadn't seen any sign of fleas on Feela—but then, I didn't know what the signs were.

"How long have you had a cat?" asked Kris, his eyes burning with need-to-know.

"I haven't got a cat!" I snapped. "I don't even know anyone who's got a cat!"

"Ah," said Kris. "So you didn't get that hair off one of your rich friends' cats."

I cursed myself. Why hadn't I used that excuse? Kris didn't know I'd lost touch with everyone on the marina.

"You might as well tell me," said Kris, "'cause I'll find out in the end."

This wasn't an empty threat. Kris was dogged, and he was also smart. Not the kind of smart that passes exams, because he was useless at reading and writing, but the kind of smart that knows what's what, that works things out, that seizes opportunities and holds on to them like a dog with a stick.

I considered the options. One was simply to tell the truth. If it had been anyone but Kris, I wouldn't have dreamed of doing this. But I knew that Kris was the last person to tell the authorities. Kris hated Comprot (as Community Protection are generally known) and they hated him. They tagged him for two years after he sprayed CHILD BEATER on the front door of Kelis Hunt's dad's house. He got the tag off, ended up in a ruck with the compers, and after that it was any excuse to pick him up. One time they threatened to have a Y-chip put in his head, and only a last-minute appeal from the Social Team stopped it.

Another thing about Kris, he never wore logos. He'd rather be seen dead than have a Nike swoosh on his cap, or a Viafara cat on his boots. No one owned him, he said, and he wasn't anybody's advertising space. I figured if he hated those companies, it was a good bet he was against the cat market.

Besides, what a relief it would be if I could tell someone else about Feela! I had so much I wanted to talk about, and it was obvious Kris knew stuff about cats. I might need that advice one day.

To hell with it—he'd find out anyway.

"OK," I said, checking that no one else was listening. "I'll tell you. But you must swear not to breathe a word of it to anybody."

"I'm not stupid," said Kris.

I took a breath. "We found it in the garden," I said.

Kris's eyes narrowed. "When was this?" he asked.

"About a month ago," I replied.

Kris raised his eyebrows. "You naughty girl," he said.

"We were going to tell the authorities," I protested. "We just got kind of . . . attached."

"I bet you did," said Kris. "Male or female?"

"Female," I replied.

"What color?" asked Kris.

"Ginger, black, and white," I replied.

"Calico," said Kris.

"Is that what they're called?" I asked.

Kris nodded.

"How come you know so much about cats?" I asked.

"Research," replied Kris.

"Research?" I repeated.

"Haven't you heard of research?" asked Kris.

"Course I have," I replied. "What kind of research?"

"Never mind," said Kris.

There was no point in trying to get the whole truth out of Kris. But no matter. He was a partner-in-crime, and I needed that partner badly. I started to pour out stories of how I'd trained her, what her habits were, how we'd hid from the Pets Inspector. Kris listened impassively, and after a while, impatiently.

"Can I see it?" he asked, interrupting me.

This, needless to say, was another matter.

"I'd have to ask Mum," I replied.

"Oh, must ask *Mummy*," sneered Kris.

"That's right," I replied. "I must."

"Got to ask permission foreverything, have you?" asked Kris.

"It's not like that!" I said. "She considers me, too!"

"Ahh," said Kris. He was starting to annoy me now. There was no reason to diss me being close to Mum, just because he was cut off from his family, and lived in a slum, and wasn't close to anybody.

"Go away now," I said. "I'll text you."

Chapter Five

Mum hit the roof when she found out I'd told Kris about Feela. The trouble was, she'd never met Kris, so it meant nothing to her when I said he'd never rat us out. I had no choice but to grant Kris's wish and invite him over, in the hope they'd get along.

As it happened, Mum was out when Kris stopped by, breezing in just as Feela was cleaning herself.

Feela's cleaning routine never ceased to amaze me. She could get her tongue everywhere on her body except the top of her head, and to clean that she licked her wrist and ran it over her ears. The whole thing gave her such pleasure that she never even noticed the two of us by the door. I glowed with pride, glancing from Feela to Kris, Kris to Feela. At first he just watched, closely, but with no expression. Then just the hint of a smile came on to his face.

"Where d'you say you found her?" he asked.

"In the back garden," I replied.

Kris nodded.

"Watch this," I said. I whistled. Feela looked up, took us in, then got back to business.

"So?" said Kris.

I was so frustrated. Feela *always* came to me when I whistled. To make matters worse, she offered up her chin as Kris sat on the sofa beside her. He began softly stroking her throat, bringing her slowly under his spell. She seemed to be so quickly at ease with him that I felt a pang of jealousy.

"She's like that because of me," I said.

"Really," said Kris.

"She really loves me," I added.

"Uh-huh," said Kris.

"Cats are just the most miraculous things," I said.

"If you love them that much," said Kris, "why didn't you just buy one?"

I seethed. "We can't afford a cat!" I snapped. "I don't know why you think we've got so much money, because we haven't! If we had money, would we be . . ."

I stopped, but Kris had already guessed what I was going to say.

"It's all right, Jade," he said. "I know you wouldn't live around here unless you had to."

I blushed. "There you go then," I said. "We certainly can't afford a cat."

Kris, typically, wasn't going to leave it at that. "Your old man must have been worth a lot," he said. "Didn't he have life insurance?"

"What's that to do with you?" I asked.

"I'm curious," he said. "Like a cat."

"There was something wrong with his life insurance," I explained. "Something in the small print."

Kris laughed out loud. "Something in the small print!" he repeated. "Better read it next time, hadn't you?"

I was getting really irked. "Yeah, well at least I *can* read," I snarled.

"I can read!" said Kris, and suddenly he looked like a wounded little boy, and I felt terrible. But Kris wasn't the type who needed sympathy. Like most people around here, his favorite means of defense was attack, and right now that meant showing me his power over my cat. He gently rubbed the area at the base of her spine, just above her tail. She lowered her head and arched her back up towards his hand, holding her tail to one side and going into a kind of ecstasy. I'd never stroked her like that, or seen this reaction, and I was starting to get very fed up.

"You've seen her now," I said. "Bye."

Kris ignored me. He was totally concentrated on Feela, rubbing harder, smiling at the effect he was having.

"Bye," I repeated.

"Not doing any harm," he mumbled.

"Yes you are," I snapped. "You're disturbing her sleep-time."

"What did you invite me for then?"

"I invited you to look at her, not to touch her!"

"What right have you got to say I can't touch her?"

"She's *my* cat!"

"What, you own her, do you?"

"Just get lost, Kris!"

At this point Mum walked in. It could hardly have looked worse—me in the middle of an argument with the person we could supposedly trust with our lives. But there was something about Kris which Mum instantly warmed to. I winced when he called her "Mrs. Jade's mum," but Mum liked a bit of cheek, and pretty soon they were sparring away as if they'd known each other years. Mum said how much she liked Kris's earrings, and Kris said how cool she'd look with a nose-ring, and I started to feel like a total fifth wheel, all the more so as Feela was still on the end of Kris's tickling finger.

Kris was doing it on purpose, that was for sure. He never bothered to charm anyone at school, hardly even smiled in fact, but here he was revealing his tombstone teeth at every opportunity. Maybe he was always like this with older women (except teachers of course), or maybe it was just a way of getting at me. Either way, I was relieved when he eventually left.

"What a nice boy," said Mum. "Why haven't you invited him around before?"

"He's not that nice, really," I replied, reclaiming my rightful place next to Feela.

"I can see he might be a bit of a devil," said Mum, "but he's good at heart."

"Dunno why you think that," I mumbled.

"He's just got a look about him," said Mum.

I ran my hand gently over Feela's head, but her eyes were still fixed on the door through which Kris had left.

"What kind of look?" I asked.

"The fires of righteousness," replied Mum.

"The *what*?" I gasped.

"Bit like your dad when I met him," replied Mum. "Before he got worn down."

I didn't bother to respond to this. If there was any similarity between Kris Delaney and my dad, it was lost on me.

"So," I said, "it's all right I told him, then."

Mum sighed. "I'd still rather you hadn't," she replied. "But if you had to tell anyone . . ."

"I'm not stupid," I said.

"No, you're like me," she said. "I always had good taste in boyfriends."

I leapt to my feet in a fit of outrage. "He is *not* my boyfriend!" I cried.

Mum laughed. "All right—good taste in friends, then!" she said. There was a pause, then, with a little smile, she added, "But I think he's got a thing for you."

"Mum," I warned. "Please shut up. You're making me feel sick."

Chapter Six

After his first visit to our house, Kris obviously felt he didn't need invitations. He was around the next day, carrying a disgusting pig's foot in a bag, which he said was a present for Feela.

"I don't think she'll eat that," I said.

"Why not?" said Kris.

"It looks horrible," I said.

"To you, maybe," said Kris, "but you're not a cat."

"I know that," I snapped.

Needless to say, Feela ate the pig's trotter, and the fish-head Kris brought the next day, and the chicken livers he brought the day after. Mum was well impressed with Kris's thoughtfulness, but I knew there was more to it than that. He just wanted to be inside my home, like a hermit crab, probably because he resented me having a home when he just moved from one place to another, from one supposed uncle to another supposed cousin, with no stability at all.

Maybe he secretly wanted to live with us. He always said he hated cozy, domestic life, and if he had his own way he'd still live on the road, but it certainly didn't bother him to sit down in front of the screen with a cup of tea, passing the time of day with Mum.

Then again, maybe he just wanted to be with Feela. For me, her appeal was that she was beautiful, and responsive, and fascinating in everything she did. But for Kris, she was what the rich people had. She was something stolen, illegal, something denied to us which we'd taken anyway—except it was me who'd taken her, and Mum who stood to go to jail if they ever found her. So Kris could have all the pleasure of her with none of the risk.

And then, to top it all off, Mum gave him a key.

I wasn't at home when it happened. I only found out about it later that evening, when Mum happened to casually drop it into the conversation.

"*What?*" I cried. "You mean he can just let himself in, any time, night or day?"

"He's not going to let himself in," replied Mum. "It's just for emergencies."

"What kind of emergencies?" I asked.

"Supposing something happened to us," said Mum. "Someone would have to feed Feela."

"Be cheerful, why don't you?" I scoffed.

"Jade, we've got to be prepared for any eventuality," said Mum. "There's no one else we can ask."

I folded my arms and scowled. "I don't care," I said. "I don't want Kris having a key to my house and *you should have asked me*!"

"*That's* why I didn't ask you," said Mum.

"There isn't going to be an emergency," I muttered.

"Please, love," said Mum. "Don't go on." She reached for her heart pills and I left it at that, hoping against hope I hadn't tempted fate by what I'd just said.

It was just three days later that Feela didn't come to wake me up. By now our routines were so settled that I immediately sensed something was wrong. I went downstairs and found her, still asleep, on top of the freezer. The food we'd put down for her hadn't been touched.

"Feela?"

I raised her chin gently on my finger. Her eyes half opened.

"You all right, kitten?"

I lifted her down, carried her through to the living room, and set her beside the sofa. She loved to sharpen her claws on the arm, no matter how much we told her off. Today, however, she barely sniffed at it, jumped weakly on to the cushion, tucked her paws beneath her breast, and closed her eyes.

Just before I was about to leave for school, Feela began making an unearthly crying sound. Then she stretched out her neck and was sick twice. Almost immediately she was asleep again, but now her breath was becoming labored. Mum and I began to fear the worst.

"We should have expected this," said Mum.

I tried to look calm and responsible, but within me was flat panic. Not just for Feela, but for myself. If this *was* that deadly disease . . .

"We've got to do something," I pleaded.

But what?

Feela, meanwhile, had climbed up onto the kitchen counter, eyes glazed forward.

"Come on, lovely," I said. "You know you're not supposed to be up there."

I reached up to take Feela down, as I'd done many

times before. But this time she reacted differently. I don't know if it was because she felt vulnerable, but she hissed like a snake and swiped at me with her paw. To my horror, I looked down to see three scratch lines across the back of my hand. As thin lines of blood began to fill them, so I began to panic.

"Mum!" I cried. "She's cut me!"

Mum purified some water and made me wash the wound. As usual she was full of sureness and common sense, but I could see the anxiety in her eyes. She'd always been more scared than me that Feela could be carrying HN51. And if this was it . . .

"You've got to get it checked out," she said.

"But they'll ask questions," I protested.

"You can say it was someone else's."

"They might need to see the cat."

"Jade, you could die!"

All Mum's hidden fears were suddenly bursting into the light. Five children had already died at our school since New Year. Not that their deaths had anything to do with cats.

"OK, OK!" I assured her. "I'll go and see the medic."

I didn't. I went to school. But I couldn't concentrate for a second, and as the hours ticked by, so my fears grew until my veins were awash with adrenaline and the panic inside me was unbearable. I felt ill—really ill. My skin felt sore and my forehead burned. Was this it? Was this the disease which could kill within a day?

I made an excuse and went down the clinic. My heart thumped in that waiting room, and by the time I got to see Dr. Amso, I was so nervous it was unreal.

"I think I need a blood test," I told him.

"I see," he replied. "And why's that?"

I listed all the symptoms I'd read about, all the symptoms I was convinced I'd now got. I didn't mention cat flu, because I was hoping he'd give me the test without trying to diagnose what I'd got. But his suspicions were obviously aroused, and when he caught sight of the scratches on my hand his manner became urgent.

"How did you get these?" he asked.

My heart began to race. "Off our roses," I replied.

Dr. Amso shook his head. "This is an animal scratch," he declared.

I flushed a little. "It must have been my rabbit," I blurted.

"Not the roses then," replied Dr. Amso.

"I was trying to get it out of the garden," I gabbled. "I

felt a scratch, and I thought it must have been the rose, but maybe—"

"What's your rabbit's name?" asked Dr. Amso.

"Bunny," I replied.

"What color is it?" asked Dr. Amso.

"Gray," I replied. "Why are you asking all these questions?"

"I don't think this scratch was caused by a rabbit," said Dr. Amso. "Do you have a cat?"

"No," I replied unconvincingly.

"You'll have to be tested," continued Dr. Amso. "I need to know if this is a cat scratch. Cat scratches are notifiable."

"What does *notifiable* mean?" I asked.

"Is it a cat scratch?" asked Dr. Amso.

By now my face was hot as a fire. "My rabbit did it!" I gabbled. "And if you don't believe me I'll find another doctor that does!"

I stormed from the doctor's office and out through the waiting room, ignoring the receptionist's demands for me to pay the check-up fee. Dr. Amso actually pursued me, right out into the street, but by then I was running. Passersby looked on, astonished. But I wasn't stopping for anyone. I thought of going home, and then another thought occurred. I would see Kris.

I'd been avoiding Kris since he'd started coming to our house every day. But today at school I couldn't have been happier to see him. He seemed to sense, as soon as he saw me, that something was wrong. We found a quiet corner behind the skate rink and I poured out my fears.

"Kris, I'm scared," I began. "Feela's sick."

Kris looked concerned. "What's the matter with her?" he asked.

"I don't know," I said. "She's just really weak, and she's not eating, and . . ." I started to tear up.

"That could be loads of things," said Kris.

"Kris . . ." I began, "I'm scared it's the flu."

"Why?" said Kris. "What do you know about cat flu?"

"Just things I've read," I replied.

"Don't believe anything you read," said Kris.

That was a typical Kris thing to say, and it didn't reassure me. "Kris," I said. "I'm scared she's given it to me."

"And why's that?" asked Kris sarcastically.

"I feel ill," I whimpered.

Kris folded his arms and viewed me with something like pity. "Jade," he said. "Humans can't catch cat flu."

"*What*?" I replied. "Of course they can!"

"Really?" said Kris. "And how do you know that?"

"Everyone knows!" I said.

"Maybe everyone's wrong," he replied.

"How do you know they can't?" I asked.

"I study the evidence," replied Kris.

"What evidence?" I asked.

"The history of the flu scare," said Kris. "It's on the Free Cats League site."

"Never heard of it," I said.

"It's on the freeweb," replied Kris.

"That's illegal!" I said.

"*Really?*" said Kris. "I better stop using it then."

"The freeweb's disgusting," I said.

"Is that what you've heard?" asked Kris.

"All the pictures of . . ." I began. "I don't like to talk about it."

"Because you've never seen it," replied Kris. "Because you know nothing about it."

"I've read about it," I said.

"Yeah, on the slaveweb!" laughed Kris. "Owned by James Viafara, head of the Viafara Corporation, the same people that own the cats!"

I paused. Kris always made me think, but I still couldn't accept that millions of people would believe a lie. James Viafara may have been rich and powerful, but he was also known to be generous and trustworthy, a man who'd raised billions for Africa. Anyway, there were scientific papers about HN51, documentaries on the telly, politicians making speeches . . .

"They wouldn't just make it all up," I said.

"Do *you* know anyone who's died of cat flu?" asked Kris.

"No . . ." I began, "but that's because cats are controlled."

"Jade," said Kris. "You're not going to die."

This I *did* want to believe, and Kris said it with such certainty the heat in my forehead seemed to ebb away a little.

"But the doctor wanted me tested," I said.

Kris's face dropped. "You went to the doctor?" he gasped.

"I was scared!" I protested.

"What did you tell him?" asked Kris.

"I just said I was feeling sick," I began. "I thought he'd give me a blood test . . . then he saw these." I showed Kris the scratches on my hand. "Feela did it this morning," I explained.

"Did you tell him that?" asked Kris.

"Course I didn't!" I protested. "But I think he guessed."

"Jade, you idiot!" barked Kris.

"Don't call me that!" I snapped.

"It's notifiable!" cried Kris.

"Yes, I know that!" I replied.

Kris slapped a hand to his forehead. "Why didn't you just ask me first?" he railed.

I saw red. "Who do you think you are?" I cried. "I don't answer to you! You don't own me! And I'll tell you this—if it had been up to me, you wouldn't have a key to my house in a million years!"

I stormed off in a fit of anger and confusion. I was angry at Kris for his arrogance, but I was more angry at myself for my stupidity. All the more so when I arrived home, opened the front door, and saw Feela happily running down the stairs.

"Panic over," said Mum. "Must have just been an upset tummy."

I dropped into the nearest chair. The adrenaline drained away like water down a plughole, and suddenly I felt utterly exhausted. What a fool I'd been!

After a while, Feela joined me. She leapt silently on to my lap and stood on my leg, facing away, like a miniature lion. I stroked her supple little back and, as was her habit, she turned her head, blinking, expecting more affection. I don't know how long we stayed there, me stroking, her purring, but it really was as if we had become part of one another. I know she was only an animal, acting on instinct, but she had come to know me, and our relationship was real. Even if she didn't consciously intend to give me happiness, I felt such peace in her company that it made me yearn for all life to be like this.

Chapter Seven

I must have fallen asleep on the sofa. The next thing I knew, there was a thunderous crash which ripped me awake with a thudding heart.

Men. There were men in the house.

Too late to act. The door to the front room smashed open, and they were in there with me—terrifying helmeted figures, lots of them, stun-stems in their hands. A single shout of "There!" and one yanked me off the sofa while the others tore it away from the wall. Then they started on the rest of the furniture.

In the midst of this nightmare Mum appeared. Immediately her hand went to her heart. I saw her dropping, the men holding her up, some violent swearing, someone jabbering into a wristphone. Then I was pinned by a vice of massive arms, face to the wall, unable to see. They held me there for what seemed ages, while boots thundered around the house, up the stairs, through the upstairs rooms, accompanied by deafening crashes and yells. Throughout it all I wouldn't stop struggling and I couldn't stop screaming. Eventually sheer exhaustion got the better of me, and I finally sank into passivity, like prey about to die. By now the immobilizer was on me and they could turn me to face them. The room was a wreck and Mum was sat dead still on the sofa, her face ashen. One of the compers had his helmet off. He had the pencil beard and moustache so beloved of the security forces. On his jacket were the words TOWARDS A SAFER CITY.

"Where's the cat, love?" he barked.

"Haven't got a cat," I replied, voice warbling with emotion.

"Want to see your mum in jail?" asked another.

I exchanged glances with Mum, who was in a state somewhere between shock and mortal terror.

"No," I replied.

"Tell us where the cat is, love," said the first officer, obviously the chief.

The truth was, I didn't know the answer to this question. Either she'd found a brilliant place to hide or somehow she'd got outside—but compers were combing the garden at this very moment and somehow, miraculously, they still hadn't found her.

That left me with a terrible dilemma. If I admitted Feela existed, they'd be back again until they found her, and that would be the end of her. Mum would still be prosecuted and I'd get a tag for sure. On the other hand, if I lied, and then they found her, the sentence would be many times worse, maybe something Mum could not survive.

I took the gamble. "You can see there's no cat," I said.

"Why's your voice shaking?" asked the chief.

"Why do you think?" I asked.

"Guilt," said the chief.

"*Your* voice would shake if someone did this to you!" I cried, near hysterical. "Look what you've done to my mum! Look what you've done to our house! Now please *get out*!"

The compers came in from the garden. "Nothing," they said.

"Taken samples?" asked the chief.

A comper held up two plastic bags.

The first officer took stock for a moment, then jabbed a finger towards me. "We know you're guilty," he said.

"And one way or another, we'll get you."

It was a horrible warning, and there was no doubt he meant it. What made it worse was it seemed so personal, like I'd got one over him and, just like a playground bully, he would pick on me till he got his satisfaction. What a vile man, I thought. I watched with pure seething hatred as he turned his back and made his way out, followed by the others, the last removing the immobilizer.

I went to the window to see half the street gathered below. As usual, they watched sullenly. A lot of them hated Comprot, others went to them all the time, like going to teacher to tell on your classmates. But all of them needed entertainment, anything to break up the boredom of their lives. There were a few jeers as the van moved off, then all eyes turned to me at the window. As you may have noticed, I am a private kind of person, and last thing I wanted was to be the center of attention. I knew they thought I was stuck up, and I knew some of them would be relishing this moment—seeing the posh people from the marina on the wrong side of the law, brought down to earth, getting what they got all the time. Well, they could think what they liked.

I closed the blinds and went to Mum. She looked dreadful.

"I'm sorry, Mum," was all I could say.

Mum could barely speak, but patted me on the shoulder as if to say "It's OK." I hugged her, gently at first, then tight. We'd come through a lot together, but nothing like this.

"I'm going to lie down," she said, eventually. Even then it took her several minutes to summon up the strength to rise, and then on unsteady feet. I put my arm around her shoulder, guided her out, then watched as she climbed the stairs with painstaking steps.

Now I had to find Feela. I checked every one of her hiding places—her places of safety when the Comprot copter came over or firecrackers went off in the street. She wasn't in any of them. I checked the garden, but our garden was small, with no exits, even for cats. I looked behind every item of furniture, inside every cupboard, and beneath every bed except Mum's bed, which was too low for a cat. Was it possible she'd run out the front door? But the compers were everywhere—they were bound to have seen her.

The shock of the raid gave way to a new panic. I'd lost her. Somehow, inexplicably, I'd lost her. With nowhere else to turn, I went out into the garden, out of Mum's earshot, and rang Kris.

"Kris," I began, shakily.

"Jade?" he replied.

"They raided us," I gulped.

"Comprot?" he asked.

"Yes," I replied. "They smashed everything! They were just so violent!"

"Welcome to the real world," replied Kris.

"They never got Feela," I said.

"Uh-huh," said Kris.

"But I can't find her, Kris!" I gabbled. "I can't find her anywhere!"

"Don't worry," replied Kris. "I've got her."

"*You've* got her?" I gasped. "How come?"

"I took her late last night," said Kris.

"What?" I cried. "You just let yourself in—"

"Don't complain, Jade," interrupted Kris. "She's alive."

I tried to take this in. "You mean," I said, "you knew they were going to raid us?"

"Didn't know," said Kris. "Guessed."

"Then why didn't you wake us and warn us?" I railed.

Kris made no reply.

"Is she all right?" I asked.

"Fine," said Kris.

"Where are you?" I asked.

"In the den," replied Kris.

"Den?" I said. "What den?"

"I'm not talking over the phone," said Kris. "I'll come and see you."

"When?"

"Tomorrow."

"What about Feela?"

"She'll be all right here for now."

The phone went dead. I started to ring him again, but thought better of it. Kris wouldn't answer. Exhausted and nerve-wracked, I went to my room and lay down, but there was no chance I'd sleep. For hour after hour I tossed and turned, replaying the horrible events I'd witnessed, worrying about Feela, rehearsing arguments with Kris, fantasizing about revenge on that vile comper.

I was relieved that Mum had managed to sleep after all that had gone on. Mum had never slept well since Dad had died, and often I'd hear her get up in the night to make a cup of tea. It was very rare she'd still be asleep when the sun came up.

As the light began to fill my room, I thought I'd better check on her.

I tiptoed down the landing and knocked softly on her door.

"Mum?"

There was no reply.

My heart began to thud. "Mum?"

Still no reply.

Anxiously, I pushed open the door. In the dim light I could just make out her shape on the bed and her shoes on the floor. Then, with mounting terror, I realized she was outside the duvet and still wearing her clothes.

I pulled open the curtain and gazed with horrified eyes upon my greatest fear.

Chapter Eight

Mum was a cautious, wise person in everything, and had prepared well for this dreadful occasion. She had an account with Bereavement Solutions, and had instructed me many times what to do in the event of her death. Those conversations came back vividly—Mum patiently explaining, me never wanting to listen, telling her she wasn't going to die, trying to change the subject from one I simply couldn't face.

Now, however, I had to face it whether I liked it or not, and like a robot I began carrying out my allotted tasks. First I rang the medical center, and waited what seemed an age before a doctor arrived, examined the body, and pronounced her dead. By now, of course, I knew this, but hearing the word from the doctor somehow made it final. I broke down in front of him, convulsed in sobs, while he reassured me in a practiced, official way, then contacted the coroner to arrange the post mortem. As he left I pulled myself back together, returned to robot mode, and rang Bereavement Solutions. Someone answered in a strange accent, probably on the other side of the world. I learned that Mum's account was silver standard, which meant there would be no dressing up of the body and, providing the post mortem was in order, the cremation would take place next day without a service. However, they would provide flowers, install a small memorial, and contact everyone on Mum's list of friends and relatives.

Numbly, I agreed to everything they said. The coroner came around at noon and did his business, recording the cause of death as heart failure. I explained everything that had happened, about the raid, the brutality, the noise, the shock. Shouldn't there be some kind of inquiry, I asked, like when you have a murder inquiry because, sure as anything, Community Protection had killed her.

The coroner told me I had the right to take the matter to court if I wished, but he advised against it. Mum wouldn't be able to be cremated, the costs would be enormous, and the chances of winning virtually zero. Since Mum had died of natural causes, it would be impossible to prove a link between her death and the

Comprot raid, especially as no one had laid a finger on her.

I didn't push it. I was still in shock and barely had the strength to stand, let alone take a case to court. As the coroner left I rang Bereavement Solutions, and less than an hour later two men came, put Mum's body in a bag, and began carrying her out of the house. At the sight of this I lost it completely. I don't even know what I was doing or saying, but I was doing and saying it long after they'd gone, and loud enough for the whole street to hear. Eventually the shock took over again and I sank on to the sofa, staring at Mum's empty chair opposite. I was utterly lost, alone, the only person on a barren planet. But worse than the loneliness was the guilt. No matter how many times Mum had said we had both chosen to keep Feela, I still felt I'd brought this upon her.

The thought of Feela was my only comfort. Suddenly she seemed like the last strand connecting me to the world. I longed to bury myself in her fur and feel the reassurance of that rich, warm purr.

Returning to life, I grabbed my phone and urgently pressed Kris's number. I'd never been happier to hear his voice.

"Kris," I said. "Where are you?"

"Chapel Street," he said. This was the street Kris used to live on, the next street down from ours.

"Where's Feela?" I said.

"Don't worry," he replied. "She's all right."

"I need to see you now," I said.

"I'll come around," he replied.

I hadn't really wanted that, but the phone went dead and five minutes later he appeared at the door. I ushered him inside.

"Kris," I said. "Something terrible's happened."

There was a flicker of deep anxiety on Kris's face. Then he seemed to steel himself.

"Mum's died," I said.

I waited for Kris to open his arms and enfold me, and at that moment, it was all I wanted. But he made no move. He said nothing. His face showed no emotion.

"Kris, my mum . . ." I repeated. "My mum's died."

"Yeah, I heard you," he replied.

"Well, say something, won't you?"

"What do you want me to say?"

"I don't know . . . I don't have to tell you, do I?"

Kris shrugged. "She's your mum," he said.

"What does that mean?" I asked.

Kris shrugged. "It means, she's your mum," he said.

"She's not mine."

I gazed at him in sheer disbelief. "What's the matter with you?" I said.

"I'm not the one who's losing it," replied Kris.

I couldn't even reply to this. Suddenly the cool I'd always admired looked like something else completely. Kris was sick.

"I want to see Feela," I said.

"You'll have to come to the den," said Kris.

"I want her here!" I cried.

"That would be mad," said Kris.

"Why?" I said.

"Because they'll be back, that's why!" said Kris. "You don't think they've finished with you, do you?"

"But then I'll never be able to have her back!" I cried.

Kris's only response was to hand me a map he'd drawn, with some instructions, written in the crude capital letters he always used. "You can come over later," he said. "Is there anything else?"

Dumbfounded, I shook my head. "See you then," said Kris. He made his way out and I watched him saunter down the street, hands in pockets, self-contained, a stranger in every way. I was hardly aware that I was standing shoeless, face streaked with tears, in full view of the neighbors. Then I heard my name and turned to see Kira, who lived opposite, rising from the chair she had parked on the pavement.

"Are you all right, love?" she asked.

There was so much concern in Kira's voice, I was taken totally by surprise. We'd exchanged a few words now and then, and I lent her a bike pump once, but other than that I hardly knew her. But seeing the look of sympathy in her eyes, I just broke down completely. I fell into her arms, too upset to feel embarrassed, and she hugged me tight.

"Is it your mum, love?" she asked.

I nodded, between sobs.

"You poor love," she said.

"What happened, love?" rasped another voice. It was Rochelle, the woman from number 8, with the deep voice and the bottle-red hair.

"They came in our house . . ." I sobbed. "They were vile to her . . ."

"Compers, is it?" said Rochelle.

I nodded.

"They're bastards," said Rochelle, in a matter-of-fact way. It suddenly occurred to me that both Rochelle's boys were tagged.

"Come over and have a beer," said Kira.

Kira led me over the road and into her house, yelling at one kid not to gawk and another to put the kettle on. We went into the kitchen to be met by a massive Alsatian.

"Hang on, love," said Kira. "I'll just get the dog out the back."

Kira grabbed the huge Alsatian by the collar and bodily dragged it past me towards the back door. "It's all right," she said. "It won't hurt you."

"Not once it's had your arm," rasped Rochelle.

I sat down amongst the toys and computer parts while Rochelle took charge of the fridge, handing me a can I had no intention of drinking. Kira returned and sat beside me.

"I couldn't believe it when I seen the compers go in your house," said Kira. "I thought they got the wrong address."

"They thought we had a cat," I replied, which was at least true.

"I bloody hope not!" said Kira. "God, I'd wet myself if I thought there was a cat across the road!"

"Even the legal ones scare me," added Rochelle.

"It was her heart, was it, love?" said Kira, changing the

subject. "I know she had a bad heart."

I was surprised Kira knew this, and wondered how much else she knew. "Yes," I said.

"Who's going to look after you now, love?" asked Rochelle.

"I don't know," I replied.

"Got no relatives?" asked Kira.

"I've got a gran," I replied. "But she's in a home."

"No aunts?" asked Rochelle.

"Two," I replied. "They're both in Australia."

"You must have *some* relatives!" said Kira.

"My dad was an only child," I replied. "Mum's got some cousins, but they were never close."

Rochelle shook her head. "They won't let you keep the house," she said. "Not on your own."

"You'll be in the warden center," said Kira. "That's where they put the strays." Her hand shot to my shoulder. "Sorry, love," she added. "It's just what people call them."

Kira didn't have to apologize. At least she didn't call the center by its other name—Suicide Hall.

To live there would be unthinkable.

"You look tired, love," said Kira. "Would you like a lie-down?"

I took up the offer. Even though Kira's place was like Waterloo Station, it was a thousand times better to be with people than alone in that house. Kira made some space in the storeroom, put down some cushions, and gave me a blanket. I thanked her over and over, feeling secretly guilty that I'd hardly talked to her before this day. Maybe the girls at school were right. Maybe I was stuck up.

I began to drift off, but the thought of Mum kept coming back, and every time I felt the same sense of disbelief, the same utter frustration at not being able to talk with her or simply be around her. For all I loved her, what hurt most was knowing I'd lost the one person who loved me, without question, utterly. Again and again the new truth smacked me in the face. I had no mum. I had no one but Feela and a friend who wouldn't even put an arm around me.

Somehow, however, I must have dropped off, because the next thing I knew, Kira was trying to wake me. "Jade!" she hissed. "Jade, wake up now!"

I pulled myself together. Kira was looking anxious.

"They're over your house, love," she said. "You'd better get out of here."

"Comprot?" I asked, dazed.

57

Kira nodded. "Must have something on you, love."

"I've got to tell them they're murderers," I blathered.

"Just take my advice and get out," said Kira. "They've come to arrest you."

Vaguely I remembered the plastic bags they'd brought in from the garden. Forensics must have found something.

"Can't I hide here?" I asked.

"No, love," said Kira. "They'll be over here next. We'll get you out the back."

I was hurried down the stairs. Rochelle was there with a little day-bag into which they'd stuffed a few things. "You may need these," she said. Kira chained up the dog and they bundled me into the backyard. At the same time there was a heavy knock at the front door.

"That's them," said Kira. "Carl!"

Carl, one of Kira's nephews, came running with a ladder. He seemed to know the score. The ladder was placed against the end wall, over which Kira yelled, "Josh!"

"Wha's happenin'?" came the reply.

"Got one coming over, Josh!" cried Kira.

"OK," came the reply.

"Over you go, love," said Kira. "Good luck."

I climbed the ladder—like many before me, obviously—and down another the other side to find myself beside a plastic paddling pool full of toddlers, greeted by a man in a Jamaica football shirt. "This way, petal," he said, leading me through the house and out onto the next street without another word.

With fumbling hands, I opened the map showing the way to Kris's den. It was the only place left to go.

Chapter Nine

I'd never been to the wasteland around the old industrial park. The place had been abandoned years before and there were rumors there was unburied nuclear waste there. It was all fenced off but, as always, kids had found a way in, and evidently so had Kris.

The den was certainly well disguised. From the outside it just looked like a bramble patch in the corner of an old parking lot. Junk was strewn all over it and if you looked hard enough, you could see a car tire buried in the middle. That car tire, according to Kris's instructions, was actually the front door.

I waded through the brambles and shouted Kris's name. Sure enough, like a submarine captain, he emerged from his turret and invited me in.

I climbed down a rope-ladder into a concrete tank, lit

by a few LED lights. The stink was awful. There were cushions, one small stool, a camping stove, a sleeping bag, and boxes which served as tables and cupboards. Over one corner of the floor there was actually some raffia matting, and there on the matting, looking expectantly upwards, was Feela.

I can't describe the surge of emotion I felt at seeing her. If anything, she seemed more beautiful than ever. I threw myself towards her and lay my head against her side. I'd used her as a pillow many times and she'd never objected, as long as I didn't put my full weight on her. Now, with that rich purr filling my ears, I felt as small as a kitten, lost in a warm presence as big as the universe. *Everything's all right*, she seemed to say. *Everything's all right.*

"Don't say hello," said Kris.

"I just needed to see Feela," I said.

"Yeah, well," said Kris. "Don't forget she's here because of me."

I raised my head and looked around. Now my eyes had adjusted, I was surprised to see how many little things Kris had done to make the place more homey. There were G-prints stuck to the walls, squares of patterned cloth on the tops of the boxes, and a ring of fairy lights around a mirror. I began to feel a little better.

"They came back," I said.

"Told you," said Kris.

"They're going to arrest me," I said.

"Not if you stay here," said Kris.

"I'm not staying here!" I said.

Kris shrugged. He told me how he and his brothers had found this place years before, turned it into a makeshift home, stayed for weeks sometimes, when there was nowhere else to go. Then his brothers had decided to play ball with the authorities and since then, he'd been the sole tenant.

"Where are your brothers now?" I asked.

Kris shrugged again. "Don't know, don't care," he said.

"You must care," I replied.

"Anyway," said Kris. "If you're not staying here, what are you going to do?"

"I don't know, I don't know," I said, dropping wearily back onto Feela.

Kris watched me a while, then quite softly said, "We got to get away, Jade."

"Why d'you say 'we'?" I asked.

"They'll be looking for me, too," said Kris.

"How do you know?" I asked.

"Just take it from me," said Kris.

I didn't pursue the matter. My mind was fixing on the thought of escape, and I wasn't going to turn down an offer of help.

"But where would we go?" I asked.

"Ireland," replied Kris.

Now I knew Kris was mad. For months the news had been full of explosions, killings, and mayhem on the streets in Ireland. It was the last place I wanted to go.

"Why on earth do you want to go to Ireland?" I asked.

"Because," replied Kris, "there's a cat amnesty in Ireland."

"What's an amnesty?" I asked.

Kris let out a deep sigh. He squatted down on his haunches and began explaining to me as if I was about four years old.

"It means," he said, "you can keep Feela there."

"How come?" I asked.

"Because they've had a bloody revolution, that's why!" said Kris. "Well, not exactly a revolution. They just elected a government which kicked all the multinationals out."

"What's a multinational?" I asked.

"Don't you know *anything*?" scoffed Kris.

"That's why I'm asking!" I replied. "If you tell me I'll know, won't I?"

"A corporation," said Kris. "A big company. Like Viafara."

I tried to take this in. "They've kicked them out?" I repeated.

"Yep," said Kris.

"They can't just do that, can they?" I asked.

"They can do what they want," replied Kris. "They're the government."

"And Viafara just let them free all the cats?" I asked.

Kris gave a short, bitter laugh. "Viafara are trying to break the government," he replied. "That's what's behind all the violence."

"I thought it was terrorists," I said.

"Well then," said Kris. "Shouldn't believe all you hear, should you?"

I scrutinized Kris's face. Did he really know what he was talking about, or just sound like he did, like most boys?

"Either way," I replied, "Ireland's not safe."

"Some areas are," said Kris. "You just need to know where to go."

Again, Kris sounded so sure. I wanted to believe him. I needed to. What other choice did I have?

"How would we get there, anyway?" I asked.

"Go to Bluehaven," said Kris, "and get a jetboat."

"Aren't there security checks?" I asked.

"Not if you go with a cowboy," said Kris. "There's tons of them around, if you know where to look."

All my life I'd been a cautious person, just like Mum. All my life I'd followed her advice and checked everything out thoroughly before making a decision. Now, however, I didn't have that option. But the thought of escape seemed a fantastic dream, and the alternative was a nightmare.

"How will we get to Bluehaven?" I asked.

Kris mimed thumbing a lift. "Only way," he said. "Too much security on the rail."

"But we can't hide Feela," I said.

Kris stood up to reveal what he'd been sitting on. It was an animal carrier, with an easy-grip handle and breathing holes in the side. I felt the weight of it. It wasn't too bad.

"Come on then," he said.

"What?" I said. "Now?"

"Sooner the better," he said.

"I can't go now!" I protested.

"Why not?" said Kris.

"Kris, my mum's just died!" I cried. "She's being cremated tomorrow!"

"You don't have to go to it," said Kris.

I could have killed him. "For God's sake!" I said. "I've got to at least say good-bye!" My voice cracked as I said it, and the heaving sobs began again.

Kris waited till I'd calmed down some, and then, more sensitively, said, "Jade, Comprot will be there."

"No they won't," I murmured, wiping my eyes. But that was just what I wanted to believe, and when I'd composed myself, I began to wonder if Kris might be right.

"They wouldn't go there, would they?" I asked.

"If they want you," said Kris, "they will find you."

I got up. "I need some air," I said. "I've got to think."

Dusk was beginning to fall as I climbed out of the den. I gazed at the sky, I don't know why, because Mum wasn't up there any more than she was down here.

"Mum," I pleaded, "tell me what to do."

Suddenly, quite clearly, I heard Mum's voice. But it wasn't a miracle. Mum's voice was inside me, just as sure as my heart, my bones, and my blood vessels. And

Mum's voice said, *Save yourself, Jade. Save yourself and save Feela.*

"I want to say good-bye," I cried.

Let your escape be my memorial, said the voice.

How this sentence came to me I did not know. Maybe the memory of a book or a poem Mum had read to me once. But come it had. And the more I thought about it, the more I realized it was exactly what Mum would have wanted. She'd have thought me an idiot to risk everything for that last good-bye.

With a new resolve, I climbed back into the den to get Feela.

Chapter Ten

We'd been waiting at the edge of the quadway for half an hour. Hitching wasn't easy these days, with all the road robberies and health scares. So I sat on Feela's carrier while Kris thumbed the trucks as they came towards us and cursed them as they went past.

"She'll wake up if we don't get a lift soon," I said.

"Don't worry," replied Kris. "She'll be in dreamland for hours."

We'd already had a row about this. Unknown to me, Kris had given Feela half a Dorma to knock her out. I was furious when I discovered this. Kris said she'd be perfectly all right, and I said how did he know since he'd never had a cat, and he wouldn't answer that. Besides, I said, Kris should ask me before he did anything to my cat. Kris came out with the usual line about Feela being her own creature and not owned by anybody. By that point I was too tired to argue any more. But it seemed we just couldn't avoid arguing.

"Ha!" cried Kris, as another truck flew by. "Wouldn't go in a Nu-Market truck if they paid me! Scabs!"

"Why d'you say that?" I asked.

"They broke the rail strike," said Kris. "Carried all the cargo."

"Is that bad?" I asked.

Kris shook his head. "What planet do you live on?" he scoffed.

"I was only asking!" I snapped. "Stop talking to me like I'm six!"

Kris's answer was to move farther away from me. As luck would have it, the next truck slowed down, pulled in, and waited for us. It just happened to be a Nu-Market, which I thought was quite amusing. Kris didn't see the funny side at all, but when it came down to it, he wasn't going to refuse a lift.

We climbed up into the cab and were greeted by a red-faced, muscular man in a yellow Nu-Market cap.

"Where you going, kids?" he asked.

"New Fishguard," replied Kris.

"I can get you to Booth City," said the driver.

"That'll do," said Kris.

I sat back and relaxed. It felt good in the cab, high above the road, with all the lights and the gadgets and the music on. The driver switched on and we moved off, smooth and silent, a machine-beast of the night.

"What's your names?" he asked, turning down the radio.

"I'm Dale," said Kris. "This is Susan."

I smiled weakly, unable to give Kris the kick he deserved.

"Susan?" said the driver. "That's an unusual name."

"She's an unusual person," said Kris.

"Can't you speak for yourself, love?" said the driver.

"Obviously not," I replied.

"I'm Finn," said the driver. "Finn the van man."

"All good, Finn," said Kris.

Finn cruised smoothly into the outside lane. Kris watched every move he made at the controls with fierce concentration.

Then Finn nodded at Feela's box. "What you got in there then?"

"Ferret," said Kris.

"Oh, aye," replied Finn. There was a few seconds' silence. It was to be the last relaxed seconds of the journey. "I used to keep ferrets," he added.

"Cool," said Kris. At the same time, he shot me a glance which said, *Oh shit.*

"Is it a jill?" asked Finn.

"It's called Ferry," I replied.

"No, a jill!" said Finn. "You know, a female."

"Oh . . . um . . ." I stammered,

"Why d'you think that?" asked Kris, quickly.

"'Cause it don't smell much," said Finn.

"You know your stuff," said Kris. "Yeah, it's a jill."

"Got a hob for it?" asked Finn.

The only hob I knew was for cooking, and he couldn't mean that—could he? Maybe it was best to let Kris field the questions.

"Think that's a good idea, do you?" said Kris.

"Got to have a hob, ain't she?" said Finn. "Die without a hob. Less she's spayed, of course."

"Had one die, have you?" asked Kris.

"Me?" replied Finn. "No, not me. I know ferrets. But I knew a guy once, his jill went into heat, kept her locked up for a month—didn't want no kits, see? Went toxic and bit the dust."

"That's sad," I said.

"So, you got a hob, have you?" asked Finn.

"Nah," said Kris. "She's spayed."

"Wise man," said Finn. "Saves a lot of trouble."

By now the light had completely faded. We were speeding down the quadway at 150 kph, as if in a dream, but one you weren't in control of, one which could go horribly wrong at any moment. Finn seemed nice enough, but there was a hard look in his eye, an illegal stun-stem under the dashboard, and a war magazine on the shelf behind me. I placed my hand on Feela's box for comfort.

"So," said Finn. "What d'you feed her?"

Kris shrugged. "You know," he said. "The usual."

"Oh, aye," said Finn. "What's that, then?"

"Come on," said Kris. "You know what ferrets eat."

"I know what *I* think a ferret should eat," replied Finn. "But other people got their own opinions."

"Such as?" asked Kris.

"Mate of mine fed his ferret dog food," said Finn. "Swore by it."

"He's in good company," said Kris. "That's what we use."

There was a short silence. "And she's all right on it, is she?" asked Finn.

"Fine," said Kris.

There was another short silence. "How long you say

you had her?" asked Finn.

Kris turned to me. "How long is it now, Sue?" he asked.

"Couple of years," I grunted.

Finn said nothing, but checked me out in the mirror. I looked away. Finn turned up the radio and sang along under his breath. The conversation seemed to have ended. We made a few more kilometers, then Finn yawned.

"Time for a break," he said.

A truck stop was just ahead. Finn pulled on to the sliproad and parked up amongst the other monsters. "Come on, kids," he said, opening the door. "I'll get you a coffee."

"I'll stay here, thanks," I replied, my hand still on Feela's box.

"Uh-uh," said Finn. "Sorry, love. I can't leave you here with all the stuff I've got. No offense, but you can't be too careful these days."

Reluctantly, I left Feela and followed Finn and Kris out of the truck, across the black tarmac glistening with drizzle, into the strange lost world of the truck stop with its fake food outlets and its sinister rest cupboards. Finn led the way into the Old London Deli, bought the coffees, then sat himself opposite us, his giant hairy forearms dominating the table.

"What's the game then, kids?" he said.

"What do you mean?" asked Kris.

"That's not a ferret in that box," said Finn.

"Yes it is," I replied unconvincingly.

Finn gave something between a snort and a snigger. "No one in their right mind feeds a ferret dog food," he said. His hard, flat-top eyes scanned first me then Kris. We made no reply. "Ferret's a predator," said Finn. "Eats every bit of an animal. Guts, organs, cartilage, bone. You feed it just meat and it'll die of malnutrition."

"We don't just feed it dog food," said Kris, but Finn wasn't interested.

"So what you really got in there?" he asked.

"Ferret," said Kris.

"Let's think," said Finn. "An animal small enough to go in that box . . . but one which you got to lie about to get a lift. I can only think of one animal that fits that description."

By now my face had letters of fire written across it, and those letters spelled GUILTY.

"Where d'you get this cat then?" asked Finn.

"What cat?" asked Kris.

"Just found it," I replied.

Kris looked daggers at me, but there was no point in lying any more. And anyway, Finn was a kind of pirate of the road, an outsider, a man with an illegal stun-stem who maybe didn't think much of the law. With any luck, I thought, he might be sympathetic.

How wrong I was.

"I really ought to turn you in," said Finn. "But as I like you, I'll offer you a deal."

"What kind of deal?" asked Kris.

"Like I said, I'll take you to Booth City," said Finn. "Except now, it'll cost you a grand."

"A *grand*?" said Kris. "Are you joking?"

Finn rose up in his seat and moved threateningly towards Kris. "Listen, son," he said. "If I do my public duty and turn you in, you're looking at ten years in a youth detention center and an ID tag for the rest of your life. You should be grateful I'm so generous."

"We haven't got a grand," I protested.

"I don't believe you," said Finn.

"Why do you think we're hitching a lift?" said Kris.

"'Cause you can't use the bloody rail, that's why!" said Finn. "Think I'm stupid?"

"We could maybe afford fifty," I suggested.

Finn snorted with derision. "Hand us your ID cards," he said. "I'll find out how much you can afford."

My hand moved instinctively to my bag. No one was going near my ID card.

"We need to talk about it," said Kris.

"You got five minutes," replied Finn. "I'm on a tight schedule."

"Come on, Jade," said Kris, getting up.

"Don't you mean Sue?" said Finn with a smirk.

Kris led the way out of the diner and through the concourse to the side door. He gave a quick glance back towards Finn then faced me with an urgent expression. "You wait two minutes then go back and say I'm in the toilet," he said. "I'll go around the back way to the truck and get Feela."

"How?" I asked.

Kris held up a smartkey. "Can't be too careful these days," he said.

I was shocked. Stealing was wrong, that was always drummed into me. But to Kris it seemed as normal as breathing.

"What'll I do when he sees Feela's gone?" I asked, getting very frightened.

"Don't go back to the truck with him. Say you need

the toilet as well. Meet me back here and we'll leg it through them woods."

Kris nodded towards the trees at the back of the truck stop. It wouldn't be hard to get lost in there, I thought. But after that?

"I'm scared," I said.

"Just do it," replied Kris.

Kris turned and walked towards the exit. Without thinking any more about it, I went back to face Finn. But the moment he caught sight of me without Kris, things started to go wrong. He leaped out of his seat and raced full-tilt from the diner as the other customers gawked in amazement. I chased after him and reached the car park just in time to see Kris emerge at the other end of the building.

Kris had no chance. Finn had fifty meters on him. And just as he reached the truck, to my utter dismay, it became apparent Finn had another key. As Kris raced hopelessly towards him and I screamed at the top of my lungs, the monstrous beast-truck lit up like a fairground, and before my horrified eyes drove off into the night, with Feela a helpless passenger.

I just cried.

"What the hell did you do?" said Kris as he arrived,

panting for breath.

"I did what you said!" I blubbed.

"Crying ain't gonna help," said Kris.

"I'm not crying to help!" I blathered. "I'm crying . . . 'cause he's got Feela!"

Another belt of emotion hit me. The sobs came like heaving waves.

"Yeah, well," said Kris. "When you're used to knocks . . ."

I turned on him in disbelief. "My mum's just died!" I cried.

Kris buttoned it. For a moment I thought he was going to put an arm around me, but it was a vain hope.

"Come on," he said. "Let's get after him."

"What?" I gasped. "How?"

Kris opened his phone. His thumb punched away as his keen brown eyes focused hard on the screen. "I put a tracker on Feela's box," he said. "We should be able to pick it up on Earthline."

Kris tapped away some more, swiveled the C-wheel, then smiled.

"Got him," he said. "Just check the likely destinations."

I dried my eyes.

"OK," he said. "Let's get a train."

"What's the point of that?" I said. "They never run on time, if they run at all."

"We'll get a bullet," said Kris.

"That'll take all our credit!" I protested.

"Then we'll get more," said Kris. "Come on."

Chapter Eleven

It wasn't easy for me to step into that bullet pod. I'd overcome my fear of them because I had to, but I could never forget the day we heard what had happened to Dad. How I'd clung to Mum that day and prayed that nothing would happen to her, except I didn't really pray, because God was dead too, as far as I was concerned. Far better to believe he didn't exist than to believe in him and hate him, or her, or it, except everyone knows that God's a man really, and a typical one at that.

Anyway, they said they'd improved the design of the pods since the accident, and I did choose to believe this, because very senior people in the government said it. Unlike Kris I still believed there were people up there who were trying their best for us.

Kris barely seemed to notice we were in the pod, or the

fantastic speed at which we were traveling. His eyes were still fixed on his phone.

"He better not hurt Feela," I said.

"Why should he hurt her?" said Kris. "He wants to sell her."

"Do you think that's what he'll do?"

"Of course he will!" said Kris. "That's guy's got con man written all over him. Ah! Got him!"

Kris tapped furiously at the phone. "He's stopped," he said. "J42."

We both glanced upwards at the list of stops for the bullet. J42 was after the next one. Kris programmed the pod to stop there.

"But what are we going to do if we find him?" I asked.

"I'm going to fight him," replied Kris.

"Are you joking?" I said.

"He's a macho man," said Kris. "He won't turn down a fight."

"Kris," I pointed out. "He's twice as big as you."

"But I'm trained in tae kwon do," replied Kris.

I viewed Kris's lean arms and slender frame. He was wiry and maybe stronger than he looked, but Finn had arms and legs like knotted iron. Tae kwon do or not, he could swat Kris into the middle of next week.

"This is stupid," I said.

"Got any better ideas?" asked Kris.

"There must be something better than fighting him," I said. "Besides," I added, "I'm a pacifist."

Kris screwed up his face in disgust. "A *pacifist*?" he snorted. "What's the point of being a pacifist?"

"If everyone became a pacifist," I said, "we'd have world peace." I knew it sounded lame the moment it was out, but it was too late. Kris seized on it like a ravenous dog.

"It's not going to happen, Jade!" he growled. "Wake up! It's not going to happen."

"It *could* happen," I protested. "Anyway, I believe in setting an example."

"What of?" sneered Kris. "Someone who likes getting their butt kicked?"

I smiled lamely.

"You saw what Comprot did to get your cat," said Kris. "What if they'd found her and put a gun to her head?"

"They didn't," I replied.

"Thanks to me," said Kris. "But what if they had?"

"They didn't," I repeated. "I'm not getting involved in arguments about things that never happened."

Kris snorted. "That's a cop-out," he said.

"I just *hate violence*, OK?" I cried.

"Then don't watch," replied Kris. He stood up, sprang into a combat position, and performed a series of quick, twisting punches.

What was going through this strange boy's mind? Was this a serious attempt to get Feela back, or just some pathetic shot at proving himself as a man? Sure, he looked like he knew something about this tae kwon do— you could tell that from the precision of his movements. But if he really thought he was going to beat Finn he was living in a movie.

The pod went into a powerful deceleration and stopped. J42. We got off. Kris rechecked his phone.

"He's at the nightmarket," he said.

"Maybe he's left Feela in the parking lot," I suggested.

"I doubt it," said Kris.

"He can't sell an illegal cat at the nightmarket," I said.

"You'd be surprised," replied Kris.

We set off through a bleak industrial area, Kris practicing moves as he walked, giving me a running commentary on the art of tae kwon do.

"This is the cat stance," he said, throwing his weight onto his back leg.

"Cats don't stand on two legs," I commented.

"Yeah, but the back legs are where the power is," replied Kris. "The back legs give the purchase. The front ones do the damage."

Kris punched a quick one-two, then swiftly kicked the air, missing me by a whisker.

"I hate this," I said.

"What are you worrying about?" said Kris. "You don't have to do a thing."

"I hate that, too," I replied.

"See, when a cat fights," said Kris, "every ounce of its strength is concentrated on the point of impact."

"I'm not listening," I replied.

"Mind and body are one," said Kris.

"Kris," I said, "he's going to kill you."

"Shut up, will you?" said Kris.

It was the first sign that Kris was more nervous than he was letting on. I let it go. Up ahead, a bright halo of orange light gave the first indication of the nightmarket. As we moved forward, gradually, like the morning sun, a glowing dome appeared above the other buildings. My heart leaped as I saw a row of trucks stretching off into the distance. Despite Kris's warnings, I found myself running towards them, desperately searching till I found the beast which had carried my cat away.

Kris was right. The cab was empty. Feela was inside the market and, if we were unlucky, already sold.

Chapter Twelve

It was a typical nightmarket, a horrible place, full of obsessed people with euro signs in their eyes. The main dome was divided into twenty or so circular carousels, with a giant screen above them all, and individual screens beside each presentation spot. Eye-bots were everywhere, like giant, silent bluebottle flies. One even came to meet us and stared for a moment with its blank white eye, as if we were up for sale as well.

We moved through the market, eyes peeled for the man who'd stolen Feela. But most of the men there were truckers, and it was hard to tell one from the other.

And then we saw him. He was emerging from the dealer's area with another man in tow. My heart skipped a beat as I saw the pet carrier hanging from his hairy fist.

Kris was over like a shot, puffed up like a swan, barring the way.

"Is he trying to sell you that cat?" asked Kris.

Finn and his customer stopped in their tracks.

"Because it's not his cat to sell," said Kris.

"It's *my* cat!" I cried, catching up.

"He's a thief," added Kris.

"OK, son, that'll do," said Finn.

"I'll fight you for it," said Kris.

Finn laughed.

"Come on, big man," said Kris. "I'll fight you for it."

Finn stopped laughing.

"Get out of here," he said.

"What's the matter?" said Kris. "Scared of fighting a kid?"

"I *will* fight you if you don't shut up," said Finn.

"Yeah, that's what I want," said Kris. "You and me, outside now."

Finn turned to his companion. "Sorry about this, Des," he said. "Picked these kids up earlier, they got sight of the cat, and . . . well, you know what kids are like these days."

"Crazy," said Finn's companion.

"I'm waiting, big man," said Kris.

"You're embarrassing yourself, kid," replied Finn.

"What d'you say, scab?" asked Kris.

Finn's manner changed. His eyes set like stone. "What d'you call me?" he asked.

"What you are," replied Kris. "A scab."

"Get outside," said Finn.

Finn pushed Kris roughly towards the exit. Kris shook himself away and sauntered ahead, still playing it cool, though by now I knew what a false front this was. Finn was angry now, very angry, and my fears were growing. But Feela was still dangling from his grasp, and I had no choice but to follow and hope with all my heart that by some miracle we would get her back.

The two of them squared up in the car park. Kris's eyes closed. He breathed slow and deep, as if summoning up some mystic force. His hands circled one another, rehearsing.

Finn lowered the pet carrier to the ground then straightened up to his full height. He looked more massive than ever, knotted muscles gleaming in the artificial light. With the trace of a smile on his lips, he beckoned Kris on with both hands.

Kris went into one of his stances. He moved forward one, two steps, then took up another stance. Another step, and he was almost within Finn's reach.

Finn waited for Kris to make the first move.

Then, quite suddenly, Kris's whole manner seemed to change.

His pose disintegrated.

His shoulders slouched.

His arms dropped to his sides.

He trotted forward like an innocent pony.

"Sorry, mate," he said.

With that, Kris whipped a stun-stem out of his belt, jabbed it into Finn's chest and sent him crashing to the ground like a sack of spuds.

"Quick," he said to me. "Get Feela."

I was still too amazed to move.

"Come on," said Kris. "Before he wakes up."

I grabbed the pet carrier while Kris fitted the stun-stem back into his belt.

"Where d'you get that thing from?" I asked.

"Same place I got the key," said Kris. "Come on."

Kris made a beeline across the car park towards Finn's truck. Before I could raise a word of protest, he was climbing up into the cab.

"Come on!" he yelled.

"You can't drive that!" I cried.

No sooner had the words escaped my mouth than the truck hummed into life.

"For God's sake!" yelled Kris. "Get in!"

There was no choice for me. I climbed aboard. Kris pulled open the carrier, checked Feela was still in there, then set off, weaving a crooked line towards the exit road.

"Are you sure you know how to drive this?" I asked.

"Been driving trucks since I was nine," replied Kris. "Then again, I wasn't brought up on the marina."

"Don't start that," I replied.

We pulled on to the quadway. Kris moved up through the gears and swung into the fast lane.

"This is stupid," I said.

"You got a better way to get to the ferry?" asked Kris.

"Kris, we won't get to the ferry!" I replied. "As soon as Finn wakes up he'll call the traffic police! Then they'll know we're on the run!"

"We'll outrun them," said Kris.

"Don't be so stupid!" I cried.

"I got Feela back, didn't I?" said Kris.

"Yes, and now we're going to lose her forever!" I cried.

Kris stabbed at the buttons on the navigator. "We'll take the next junction," he said. "They'll never find us if we're off the quadway."

"I can use a navigator," I said. "Let me do something."

Kris ignored me. "That's funny," he said. "It's giving me a No Entry."

"Maybe the road's closed," I suggested.

"I can see from here it isn't," said Kris.

"It wouldn't say it for no reason," I replied.

"Nah, the firm's probably reprogrammed it," said Kris. "Maybe they don't let him use toll roads or something."

"It doesn't look like a toll road," I said.

"Soon find out," said Kris. With that, he pulled into the exit lane. We left the quadway and hit an old A-road. I relaxed a little, unhooked the lid of the carrier, and peered inside.

Feela was awake. Her beautiful head turned up towards me, and she let out a little plaintive mew. The poor thing was still groggy, and rocked a little as she tried to rouse herself up. I stroked her head softly and whispered a few words of comfort. She settled back down and I closed the lid.

"Feela's waking up," I said.

"That's funny," said Kris. "I'm going to sleep."

"You'd better pull over then," I suggested.

"No way," said Kris. "We're going all the way to the ferry. Tonight."

No sooner had Kris uttered these words than there was the most terrifying metallic shriek. We both jerked forward in our seats as the truck suddenly decelerated and Feela's carrier smashed into the front of the cab. The shrieking continued till we came to a dead halt.

"Shit," said Kris.

I ripped open Feela's carrier and saw to my relief that she was still in one piece. It was only then I realized that we were inside some kind of tunnel, with bricks looming up outside the window.

"What happened?" I gasped.

"Don't understand it," said Kris. "There was loads of room under that bridge."

"But Kris," I said, "the back of the truck's higher than the cab."

"That's true," said Kris.

"What are we going to do now?" I asked.

"I dunno about you," said Kris, "but I'm going to get some sleep."

Chapter Thirteen

We stood before the Chestnuts Guest House and pondered the options.

"Maybe we should just camp out," I suggested.

"I'll be dead if I don't get some decent sleep," said Kris.

A spot of rain fell. Then a few more.

"What are they going to think?" I asked.

"They can think what they like," said Kris. "We're paying, that's all they care about."

"But what's it going to look like?" I continued. "Two kids, just one bag between them, and a pet carrier."

"I'll hide the carrier," said Kris.

"How are you going to do that?" I asked.

"Leave it under the bush here," said Kris. "Then, once we've got the room, nip out and fetch it."

"The room?" I replied. "Don't you mean 'rooms'?"

"We can't afford singles," said Kris.

"It's my money!" I replied.

"*You* can't afford singles then," said Kris.

A slight panic took hold of me. "I'm not sharing a bed," I said.

"What makes you think I want to share a bed with you?" said Kris.

"I'm just saying," I replied.

"Well now just go and ring the bell," said Kris.

I did so. There was a long wait, then a shadow appeared behind the patterned glass of the door. The door opened and there stood a woman, about fifty, wearing a formal gray dress, with an old-fashioned bob hairstyle which seemed glued to her head. She had a suspicious look in her eye and nervously stroked the palms of her hands together, like a bluebottle fly.

"Yes?" she said in a clipped, cold tone.

"Have you got a double room, please?" I asked.

Mrs. Bluebottle's eyes darted from me to Kris and back again. "Double or twin?" she asked.

"What's a twin?" I asked.

"Two beds," she replied.

"Yes—that, please," I said.

"I've got a room on the second floor," she said.

Mrs. Bluebottle held open the door for us to enter. I could tell she didn't like the look of Kris one bit, but there was nothing unusual in that. We walked through the hall, where I was dismayed to see a copy of the *Daily Mail*. No paper printed more cat scare stories than the *Mail*.

Mrs. Bluebottle, who told us her name was Hurst, led us up the stairs and showed us the room. It was small and old-fashioned, with pine furniture, yellow walls, and blue curtains. There was a cramped shower and toilet unit off to one side, and a window with a view over next door's roof. But it was clean and it would serve our purposes for the night.

"We'll take it," I said. Mrs. Hurst insisted on payment up front. She handed me a key, gave Kris another once-over, wiped her hands together, and left.

"Cozy," said Kris, in a sarcastic voice.

"Better than most," I replied.

"I wouldn't know," said Kris.

I sat on the bed and, without thinking, took out my phone. The first thing I did, whenever I arrived somewhere, was to ring Mum. Once again that utter loss hit me in the guts, and I burst out crying.

Kris stood there above me, silent and unmoving. He

could have put an arm around me, or said a few kind words, but he did neither. After a while, when it was obvious my sobbing was not going to stop, he told me he was going to get some fish and chips and would bring Feela in when he came back.

I was starting to really hate that boy.

Chapter Fourteen

Feela must have come back to life sometime in the night. I'd nodded off for a while, then had a bad dream, then awoke to the real-life nightmare. As I lay quietly sobbing, I saw the tips of her two ears above the edge of the bed. As always, there was a few seconds' pause, then she leaped silently up beside me and stretched her face towards mine. She was responding to my distress, I knew it. Not understanding my emotions maybe, not feeling compassion, but responding all the same, just as she would to the cries of a kitten. When I didn't move, she advanced a tentative paw, and touched me gently on the cheek. That was the sign for me to stroke her, which I did, smoothing her warm head with my hand as she angled herself to get my fingers under her chin.

My sobs subsided. An ounce of calm had returned to my life. Beyond Feela I could see Kris sleeping, curled up like a baby. Kris looked a lot better asleep—neither hard nor arrogant, but young and uncertain, with long soft lashes and a mouth that twitched with his dream-thoughts, like little winces. I almost felt like protecting him; as if he'd ever let me do that. There was a reason he was as he was, and I had to give some allowance for that. Mum had liked him—that was what mattered most.

"It'll be all right, Feela," I said, more to me than to her. With that I must have drifted off again, because the next thing I knew, someone was hammering at the door.

"Are you awake?" asked a familiar female voice.

"Yeah?" I grunted.

"Ten to nine!" called Mrs. Hurst, who sounded oddly friendly. "Don't miss breakfast!"

There was no chance of that. Bleary and weary, we took our places in the dining room, having taken care to lock the door and switch on the soundgarden to cover any cries from Feela. It was Mr. Hurst who served us, a cheery, red-faced man in a striped apron. But there was something false about his mateyness, especially when he pulled up a chair and joined us for a cup of tea.

"So, do your mums know you're here?" he asked brightly.

I welled up.

"Her mum's just died," explained Kris.

"Oh, I am sorry," said Mr. Hurst.

"We're on our way back from the funeral," added Kris.

"Ah," said Mr. Hurst. "On your way back from the funeral, is it?" He gave an anxious glance at the door—why, I had no idea.

"Shall we be off?" said Kris to me.

"I'll have to get you to sign the book first," said Mr. Hurst.

It seemed puzzling to me that we were signing the visitors' book now, rather than the night before, but I let it go. Mr. Hurst brought the book to us, handed me a pen, and watched closely as I invented a name and address. Kris did the same, carving it out slowly, as he wasn't much of a writer.

"We better go now," I said.

"Just a moment," said Mr. Hurst. "I don't believe you've had a receipt."

This was getting very tedious. We waited another few

minutes while Mr. Hurst fetched us said receipt, drew us into a conversation about the weather, and had just started another one about the price of bread, when Mrs. Hurst appeared at the dining-room door. The two of them exchanged glances. Kris had really had enough by now, and made a quick good-bye. I followed shortly after, and found him on our landing in an aggravated state.

"Door won't open!" he hissed.

"What d'you mean?" I replied.

"I mean, the door won't open!" he repeated, demonstrating the point by pressing the smartkey repeatedly against the lock.

"There's another lock," I said, pointing to the old-fashioned key-lock lower down the door.

Kris let out a snort, then turned on his heels and thundered down to the first floor, where Mr. and Mrs. Hurst were waiting.

"Let us in our bloody room!" he bellowed, just as I arrived on the scene.

"I knew you two were up to something," replied Mrs. Hurst.

"You don't just go into people's rooms!" I barked.

"I do if I suspect a crime's being committed," replied Mrs. Hurst.

"That's *our* things in there!" yelled Kris.

Mrs. Hurst folded her arms and adopted a smug expression. "I don't think everything in there belongs to you, do you?" she said.

"That cat is mine!" I cried.

"We'll see if the authorities agree," replied Mrs. Hurst.

"They're on their way," chimed in Mr. Hurst.

We were in a desperate situation. A few days before, I'd have panicked. Now my mind was focused. I stretched out my hand to show the scratches. "Do you see those?" I asked.

"Scratched you, has it?" said Mrs. Hurst.

I smiled. "She's got the flu," I said.

An anxious frown came over Mrs. Hurst's face.

"And now," I continued, "so have I."

I moved towards Mrs. Hurst. She stepped back.

"Open that door," I commanded, "or I'll cough in your face."

"You've not got the flu," said Mrs. Hurst weakly.

"Don't you read the papers?" I asked. "It's everywhere! Illegal cats! Dying people! People like me, with nothing to lose!"

"Comprot will be here soon," said Mr. Hurst.

"Yes, but that'll be too late for you!" I replied.

I moved another step closer.

"Want to risk it?" I said.

I stared, unafraid, into Mrs. Hurst's face, and saw the fear in her eyes.

"Give them the key, Brett," she said.

Chapter Fifteen

Kris's head appeared from the window of the narrowboat. "Come on," he said. "We're in."

I pushed Feela's carrier on to the roof of the boat and clambered on board.

"I wouldn't leave that up there," said Kris, indicating the carrier. "Roof's rotten."

I took the carrier down. "Are you sure this thing is seaworthy?" I asked.

"Probably not," said Kris. "Lucky we're not going on the sea."

That was true. The plan was to get as far up the canal as it was navigable, which Kris reckoned was about eighty kilometers. It was slow, but it was safer than hitching another ride or trying to smuggle Feela on to the rail. And it was a lot less tiring than walking, which we'd been doing for the past two hours.

"Stinks," I said as Kris let me into the long, narrow cabin, which was in a sorry state.

"No one's been on here in a while," replied Kris.

I examined the filthy seating and a few cupboards containing nothing but a broken kettle.

"How d'you think it got here?" I asked.

"Dumped, probably," said Kris.

"Why would anyone do that?" I asked.

"Probably abandoned," said Kris. "Owners thought not worth fixing it up, too expensive to moor, too expensive to scrap, dump it."

"People have no responsibility," I said.

"Yes, miss," said Kris, smiling.

"Well they haven't," I replied.

There was a long, low mew from the carrier. "She needs the toilet," I said.

"Don't let her do it in the box, for God's sake," said Kris.

I opened the carrier. Feela's head came out but she made no further move. She was taking stock of her surroundings.

"Aren't we going to start?" I asked.

"Not till I find the engine," said Kris.

"*What?*" I said.

"Don't panic," said Kris. "The main motor's gone, but these things always have a back-up."

"How do you know?" I asked.

"How do I know everything?" replied Kris smugly.

"I don't know," I replied.

"I don't waste my time reading books," said Kris.

Kris got back to work in the engine room. I hated the way he made me feel useless, except, I *was* useless most of the time. But it was thanks to me that we'd escaped the guest house, and Kris had admitted then I'd been street smart, as he put it. When he'd said that it had made me glow, like when Dad used to praise me. I didn't *want* to glow, and I didn't show it, but I couldn't deny how I'd felt and the fact I wanted to feel like that again.

For now my job was to take care of Feela, encourage her out of the carrier, and make her a litter box to go in. I succeeded at all of these things, with the help of an old tomato box and some booklets scattered around. Feela began tentatively exploring the space inside the boat, poking her nose into all the corners, testing and sniffing. At every little noise her head would jolt, and you could tell by her low stance and slow creep how nervous she was. I wished so much I could explain what we were doing, but that wasn't an option. Hopefully, when this was all over, we'd be able to give her some security again.

Meanwhile Kris was getting very frustrated. I joined him at the controls as he rummaged beneath the steering gear.

"I can't find the spare motor!" he said.

"That's because it's a battery," I replied.

"Never," he said.

"You'll find it here," I said, opening the cabinet above our heads.

Kris stared at the large oblong box I'd uncovered. "How did you know that?" he asked.

I held up the instruction booklet I'd found when I was making Feela's litter. "Read it in a book," I said.

Kris looked as hurt as if I'd stolen his favorite toy. "How do we connect it then?" he asked.

I checked the booklet. "The red and blue wires," I explained, "to the red and blue terminals."

Kris followed these instructions and the rest of the orders I gave for starting the boat, and was surprisingly gracious about it.

"I'll go home, shall I?" he said. "You don't need me anymore."

"You still have your uses," I replied. "Now get on and steer the boat."

"Yes, miss," said Kris. "Please, miss?"

"Yes, Kris?" I replied.

"Aren't you going to cast off the rope first, miss?" said Kris.

"I was just going to do that," I replied.

Kris's honor was satisfied. Despite all our trials, we'd somehow got ourselves into a good mood, and as we set off in the morning sun, it felt for just a moment like a holiday, like the way the world should be. On battery power, the narrowboat cruised almost silently down the ancient canal, Kris at the tiller, me whisking Feela's warm belly, birds twittering, no hassle, no pain.

After a while Kris started to feel tired and suggested I take over at the tiller. That was a vote of confidence, I thought. After a few instructions I took charge, which was a lot easier than I expected, except you had to think ahead, because it was a big, long boat which took time to respond. I even took the boat through a tunnel while Kris snoozed happily, ignorant of the danger he was in. When he finally emerged, bleary-eyed, he couldn't believe how far we'd traveled without crashes, sinkings, or even a bump against the canalside.

"How's Feela?" I asked.

"I thought she was out here with you," said Kris.

"*What?*" I cried.

I ordered Kris to take over at the tiller and rushed into the cabin. No sign of her. I scattered cushions left and right, opened and slammed cupboard doors, and finally, with huge relief, located her beneath the sink. But my furious search had obviously frightened her and as I reached for her, she lashed out and ran. Before I knew it she was out of the cabin. I screamed at Kris to stop her from going overboard and as he spread his arms to herd her back she panicked even more, ran straight up the cabin door, and took to the roof. Once there, there were no more escape routes, so she got as far away from us as possible and crouched warily.

"Leave her," I said to Kris.

"She can't stay up there," replied Kris.

"Just let her settle," I advised.

Feela did settle, but not for a long while, and despite all our attempts to offer her treats, she showed no sign of coming down.

"I could try and get her," I suggested.

"Roof's too rotten," said Kris. "You'll go straight through."

There was nothing to do but hope she'd get hungry. But Feela never got very hungry when the sun was out, and as the day wore on it was getting hotter and hotter. Far from wanting to move, Feela was getting more settled in the warm spot she'd found. She started lazily cleaning herself, first licking her paw and running it over her eyes, then falling back, lifting a leg, and licking that. After that she started working quite intensely on her private parts except, being a cat, they weren't that private—and little did we know it, but they were about to get very public indeed.

We'd just rounded a bend. At first it looked just like another line of trees. Then, suddenly, we realized we were running alongside the garden of an old-fashioned canalside pub, with old-fashioned picnic benches and a whole host of customers eating their lunches.

Narrowboats can't turn. We had no choice but to sail right by the customers, with Feela on full display, still busily at work on her nooks and crannies.

At first people seemed pretty amused to see us. Quite a few waved. Then, as they viewed Feela more closely, their attitudes changed. The waving stopped. Faces became serious. And just as we were leaving the garden behind two people stood up, left their pints and lunches, and came running after us.

I shouted a warning to Kris. He steered the narrowboat across to the other side of the canal, but this didn't put off our pursuers. They were a man and a woman, probably in their twenties, maybe the type who liked to make citizens' arrests or even worked as civil assistants to Comprot. Catching up with us (which wasn't hard, given our speed) they yelled at us to pull over and stop, but they were wasting their breath. Luckily enough they were running out of towpath, and had to go scrambling up a bank as we went under a bridge and out of their sight.

The reprieve didn't last long. Not far past the bridge they appeared again, running through a wood and down to the water's edge. There was no path here, but that didn't stop them from trampling the thistles and sweeping back the knotweed to get close to us.

"Jade!" cried Kris. "Get the stun-stem!"

I didn't move. Kris was just testing me, knowing I was a pacifist. As long as we stayed on the other side of the canal our pursuers could do nothing, unless they had grapple hooks under their shirts, which seemed unlikely.

"Jade!" yelled Kris. "Get it *now!*"

"They can't get us!" I cried.

"Look ahead!" yelled Kris.

I did so. Just fifty meters away the canal narrowed dramatically to become a channel scarcely wider than the boat. It was an aqueduct, and along one side of it ran a towpath—the wrong side, as far as we were concerned.

We were trapped.

I had to make a decision, maybe a life or death decision, for Feela.

I fetched the stun-stem.

Meanwhile, the man and woman had gotten ahead of us and were waiting at the aqueduct. Feela had settled now, eyes closed, within snatching distance of the towpath. But if they wanted her they'd have to get through me first. I'd taken up position at the front of the boat, where I could see the whites of their eyes.

"Get away!" I warned, jabbing the stun-stem towards them.

The woman raised both her hands. "It's OK!" she said. "We're not going to hurt you!"

I kept my guard up and my eyes fixed on the pair of them. "Get away!" I repeated.

"It's all right, Jade," said the man. "We're friends."

This, needless to say, took me completely by surprise.

"How do you know my name?" I barked.

"We've been following your story," said the woman.

My guard dropped a little. They sounded sincere. As we drew level, the man held up a leaflet. I read the words FREE CATS LEAGUE.

"Keep 'em off!" yelled Kris.

"It's OK, Kris!" I called back.

"All right, Kris?" shouted the man.

"Who the eff are you?" yelled Kris.

"I'm Raff," shouted the man. "This is Amelie. We want to help."

"Stop the motor, Kris," I said.

Kris came up level with the couple and they handed him a leaflet. He studied it for a moment, then slowed the boat. "How d'you hear of us?" he asked.

"It's all over the web," said the woman, Amelie.

"Not the papers, I hope," said Kris.

"Not yet," said Amelie.

"Jump on board," said Kris.

Amelie and Raff stepped on to the back of the boat, I joined them, and we all shook hands. Now that we'd got over the shock of meeting this couple, I trusted them totally. Mum always said I was a good judge of people, and these two had open faces, honest faces. Amelie had a rough clump of auburn hair and striking hazel eyes, dark and hooded, above a wide, red mouth full of strong teeth that looked as if they'd happily chew on a mammoth's leg—raw, if possible. Her voice as she chatted to Kris was deep and husky, with a loud dirty laugh breaking out every so often.

"We were just chatting about you," she said, "and then there you were! It was like fate!"

"Except we don't believe in fate," said Raff. He was actually shorter than Amelie, with long blond braided locks and a warm natural smile like a great slice of melon.

"She's *beautiful*," said Amelie, looking across the roof of the cabin at Feela. "How long have you had her?"

"Four months," I replied. I gave them a summary of the story so far, except once I got to Finn, they knew the rest. I couldn't believe there were people about who were actually on our side—but according to Amelie, there were plenty.

"You need to lie low for a while," she suggested.

"You can stay with us for a bit," added Raff.

"Yeah, stay with us!" said Amelie enthusiastically. "If you moor up at Strandon Locks, I'll get someone to give us a lift to our place."

"What d'you think, Kris?" I asked.

Kris shrugged. He'd gone kind of quiet since Amelie got on the boat, and I had a funny feeling he might just fancy her. For some strange reason, this unsettled me.

Chapter Sixteen

You wouldn't call Amelie's flat homey. Computers and leaflets and megaphones littered the place, so there was hardly room for furniture, and the furniture was pretty basic. But Amelie and Raff weren't the kind of people who cared about home comforts. As we soon discovered, all they cared about was cats, cats, and ending the market in cats.

Feela had never had so much fuss. One friend after another paid a visit, and every one of them was enraptured. They were quite struck on me and Kris as well. Everyone wanted to shake our hands, tell us what a great stand we were making, and wish us luck. I found this really daunting. I didn't want to be anyone's hero. I didn't want their hopes resting on me. I just wanted to get somewhere safe.

Kris, on the other hand, seemed quite happy with the attention. He recounted all the stories of our flight so far, and every time he seemed to add a new detail, till the reality was getting lost in a legend of Kris's own making.

There was a lot of discussion. Much of this centered on Ireland. Amelie didn't think much of the new government there. If they were against Chen and Viafara and the market in cats, why did they make sure the free cats were neutered? If the cats couldn't mate they'd eventually die out and we'd be back to square one.

Kris agreed with Amelie. He was even against having to take the cat to a clinic. If people couldn't really catch cat flu, why didn't the government just say it? Why did they give way to Chen and Viafara and make out there was still a threat?

I listened to the arguments but made no comment. I just didn't know the truth about anything, and it amazed me how everyone else could speak so confidently when surely they didn't know much more than me. Or maybe they did. I didn't know about that either.

The discussions turned to what we should do next.

"It's probably best to lie low for a while," said Amelie.

"It's OK to stay here," added Raff. "You should be

all right here."

That suited me. I badly needed a rest, and I badly needed to be around older people, especially a woman like Amelie, who may have only been twenty, but was canny and solid, like Mum.

"OK," said Kris. "We'll do that."

"Do I have any say in this?" I asked.

Kris gave a quick glance to Amelie. "Sorry, Jade," he said. "What do *you* think?"

"I think we should stay," I replied. "But not too long."

Kris nodded thoughtfully. "You're the boss," he said.

I tried not to laugh.

"Good," said Amelie. "We'll fix you up with beds, then when you're ready to go, we'll get the van out."

"You'll take us to Ireland?" I asked.

"Why not?" said Amelie. "Have you got other plans?"

"No," I said. "It's just that I don't want anyone else getting in trouble on account of us."

'We're not planning on getting caught," said Raff.

"Speaking of which," said Amelie, "what are we going to do about your appearance?"

"How do you mean?" I asked, all my insecurities suddenly rising.

"Your pictures will have gone out to every Comprot

force in the country by now," explained Amelie.

Kris's face dropped. "I'm not cutting my hair!" he cried.

Amelie laid a hand on his shoulder. "You don't have to," she said, reassuringly. "I'll do it for you."

Something strange happened to Kris with Amelie's hand on his shoulder. He went all quiet and tame and kind of limp. An almost silly smile appeared on his face. He muttered something about Samson then offered no further resistance.

"Now," said Amelie, looking me square in the face. "What are we going to do with you?"

I'd always hated people looking at me closely. There was a bump on my nose, my cheeks were too fat, and my ears stuck out. Mum always said I was beautiful but she was Mum, and she wouldn't be saying it anymore, and I had to try not to think about that, at least till I was on my own again.

"She'd look better without the fringe," said Kris. It was the first time he'd ever commented on my appearance, and it made me flush up.

"Yeah, let's make her look more radical," said Raff, with a grin.

The thought of this horrified me. All my life I'd tried

to look as unnoticeable as possible. I kept my hair a mousy-brown page boy, never wore make up and dressed middle-of-the-road. Maybe it was boring but I felt comfortable like that.

"Can't you just dye my hair?" I asked.

"I was thinking of braids," suggested Amelie.

"Braids would be good," said Raff.

"Don't worry," said Amelie, "we'll dye it as well."

They waited for my reaction, but I was just too petrified to speak.

"It is up to you," said Raff.

I steeled myself. "OK," I said.

I suppose there was a funny side to it. They were going to make me stand out so Comprot wouldn't notice me.

The make over began early that evening. They decided to henna my hair first, so I sat under a clingfilm helmet packed with hot mud watching Kris have his curly locks removed. Raff did this with an electric cutter, like shearing a sheep, so Kris didn't even get the compensation of Amelie's tender touch. At the end of it he gazed in the mirror with something like despair. Suddenly he looked so much younger, and more vulnerable, which was probably why he hated it. They even found him a pair of neutral glasses, so he ended up looking like a swot from the marina. I couldn't help but laugh.

"Shut up," said Kris, and he looked so hurt it made me laugh all the more. But I actually liked the way he looked now. Kris had strong eyes, quite startling, and they stood out all the more in his new choirboy face.

Now it was my turn. They washed off the mud and dried my hair. It was a bright auburn, but they'd forgotten my eyebrows, which were still a mousy brown. I looked ridiculous. Kris laughed his socks off.

"No worries," said Raff. "I'll put the kettle on again."

"No," said Amelie. "Let's do her eyebrows dark."

"No!" I cried. Didn't I look bizarre enough already?

"Trust me," said Amelie. "It'll look great."

I was not convinced. But Amelie obviously had a vision. She was as alert and excited as Feela at the sight of a bird. "You've got this pale skin," she said, "and green eyes. If we give you dark eyebrows now, you'll look kind of . . . Hungarian."

"Is that good?" I asked.

"Well, I think it'll be beautiful," said Amelie.

I somehow doubted it, and wasn't even sure if I wanted to be beautiful, but if I was, it would certainly change my appearance. So I gave way, and Amelie started work on my hair while Raff carefully applied the dye to my eyebrows. It felt nice, all this attention, especially after two days with Kris. Maybe the world without Mum wasn't such a bleak place after all.

Eventually it was done. Amelie added some loud earrings, then she and Raff surveyed their handiwork. They were delighted with it.

"What do you reckon, Kris?" they asked.

Kris nodded. "Radical," he said. He wasn't going to sound too excited, but I could tell he was looking at me with new eyes.

Raff fetched a mirror.

Oh my God.

Was that me?

It wasn't just the braids, or the new hair color. There was a new look in my eyes, sharper, older, more alive somehow. I'd been so involved in our flight I hadn't looked in a mirror in two days, and now that I did, I was a different person.

Funny enough, I think Mum would have loved my new look. She always loved it when I dressed up, or performed, or made myself special in any way. It wasn't for Mum that I hid myself.

"Now you'll pull off tomorrow night," said Raff.

"Tomorrow night?" I replied. "What's tomorrow night?"

"Didn't we mention the party?" asked Raff.

Kris's ears pricked up. "What party's this?" he said.

"Friend of ours is leaving," said Amelie. "She's having a farewell to-do on her farm."

"Will it be safe?" asked Kris.

"Sure," said Amelie.

"Will it be all older people?" I asked.

"Nah," said Raff. "Some of them will be bringing their kids."

"Teenage kids," Amelie quickly added.

"Unless you'd rather get going tomorrow," said Raff.

"No, no," said Kris. "We'll stay." Then a thought seemed to strike him. He looked quickly at Amelie, then added, "That all right with you, Jade?"

"You're the boss," I replied.

Chapter Seventeen

That night I slept on some cushions in the lounge. By now I was so tired I could have slept through an earthquake—but they say a child's cries will always wake a mother, and I was the same with Feela. The sun had only just risen when she began to make the most unearthly mewl, one I'd never heard from her before. There was a meow which meant she wanted milk, a meow which told me she wanted the toilet, and a meow which simply said hello. This meow was longer, lower, and more plaintive than any of those. It worried me.

I got up. Feela was rolling on the rush matting, rubbing her head repeatedly against it. She stretched herself out, flexed her claws, then rubbed her head against a chair leg, getting more and more frenzied. Her mewls were getting louder and longer until I was sure she'd wake the whole flat and the neighbors as well.

All kinds of thoughts and fears came to me. Was this something to do with us moving all the time? Was she so unsettled it had driven her mental? Or how about that toy Raff had given her which she liked so much—did it contain catnip? I'd heard catnip could make cats behave in the strangest ways, like people on drugs. Could it damage her brain cells?

I decided to wake Kris, who was asleep on the kitchen floor.

"Kris," I whispered. "You'd better have a look at Feela. She's acting strange."

Kris was none too pleased to be woken up, but at the sight of Feela the trace of a smile came on to his face.

"Do you know what's up with her?" I asked.

"She's got the call," said Kris.

"The call?" I repeated. "What do you mean, 'the call'?"

"She's in heat, dimwit," replied Kris.

Kris bent down and tickled Feela under the chin. This threw her into instant ecstasy, which turned Kris's smile into a long, gentle chuckle. "Y'all right, lovely?" he cooed.

I couldn't help but notice Kris's hands. I'd never realized how long and delicate his fingers were, like a squirrel's.

You'd almost say his hands were feminine, except there was hair on the back of them, and I knew how strong they were. Kris seemed contradictory in every way—both beautiful and ugly, male and female, warm and cold. There was such care and softness in the way he handled Feela, yet with me . . .

Almost as if he realized what I was thinking, Kris withdrew his hand. Feela stood up, went to the window, and mewled back over her shoulder at us.

"No way out there, lovely," said Kris.

Suddenly I remembered the conversation about ferrets. "If she doesn't mate," I asked, "could it kill her?"

Kris shrugged. "Dunno," he said.

"You must know," I said.

"I don't know everything," he replied.

"You amaze me," I said.

"I know that," he replied. He lifted his sleepy eyes to mine. There was the trace of a challenge in them.

"You look about six with that haircut," I said.

"Better than having a mental age of six," said Kris.

"Why?" I said. "What's that like?"

Life on the run had obviously sharpened my wit, and funny enough, I think Kris quite liked it. That was what it was like with him and Mum, sparring all the time.

"I don't think this is a time for joking," he said.

By now Feela was pacing up and down in front of the window like a caged lion.

"We'd better get Amelie," I said.

As soon as Amelie saw Feela she fetched Raff, and as soon as Raff saw her he fetched Tom and Gerda who were also staying. The four of them watched Feela with identical open-mouthed smiles.

"This is too good to be true," said Amelie.

"It is?" I replied.

"You've got a breeding female," said Amelie.

"Is that unusual?" I asked.

"There's a few around," replied Amelie, "but most of the free cats were originally Viafaras, so they're all neutered. At a guess I'd say Feela's been sprung from a breeding center."

"I wonder who did that?" I said.

"No way of knowing," replied Amelie. "There's been a few attacks on the centers, but they've kept them out of the news."

"What will happen if she doesn't mate?" I asked anxiously.

"How do you mean?" said Amelie.

"Could it kill her?" I asked.

"I don't suppose it'll do her any good," replied Amelie.

"What shall we do?" I asked.

"What do you think, Raff?" asked Amelie.

"Thumper," said Raff, with a wide melon grin.

"I was thinking that," said Amelie.

"Eh?" I said.

"We know someone with a tom," said Raff.

This, needless to say, came as something of a surprise. "Will it be safe?" I asked.

"Safe for which one?" asked Raff. The others laughed.

"Thumper's not a very dominant male," explained Amelie.

"He'll probably run like hell when he sees Feela," added Raff.

I had to make a decision, and soon. I didn't really want to be saddled with a pregnant cat, but I couldn't leave Feela in this state. It was too late to get her neutered now, and in any case, the vet was not an option.

"When can Thumper get here?" I asked.

"This evening," replied Amelie.

"But what about the party?" blurted Kris.

"Don't worry," said Raff. "I'll stay here and look

after things."

"Are you sure, Raff?" said Amelie.

"I'm sure you'll enjoy it much more without me," said Raff, with a knowing wink.

Chapter Eighteen

The jeepster's wheels squealed around the field for the third time, with everyone laughing but me. Even though we were kilometers from anywhere, I was still afraid of doing anything which might attract the attention of Comprot. But mercifully Tom had had enough of showing off and pulled to a halt, allowing us to get out.

At least twenty more vehicles were in the field, and the thump of music told us a big party wasn't far off. Sure enough, we soon found an open barn full of dancing bodies, with bit-screens on all sides showing living wallpaper off the freeweb. Everyone knew Amelie, who introduced us all. Even though I was dressed to the nines (in borrowed clothes) I didn't want to draw attention to myself, but everyone seemed to know who we were anyway. Since they were all Free Catters, we were soon bombarded with questions about Feela which Kris was only too keen to answer.

I took the first opportunity to hide myself behind the refreshments table, where Amelie was already helping herself from a steaming punch bowl.

"Want some, Jade?" she asked.

"Is there alcohol in it?" I replied. I'm not pretending I had never had a drink, but I didn't like the effect of it and was determined to stay in control.

"Oh, I should think so," said Amelie, with a grin.

"Just a tiny bit then," I replied.

Amelie ladled me out almost a full cupful, watching it with hungry eyes. She hadn't been out for a while and I could tell she was really up for this party.

"I hope Feela's all right," I said, taking a sip.

"She'll be fine with Raff," said Amelie matter-of-factly.

How fantastic, I thought, to have a boyfriend you could just rely on like that. Or anybody. I glanced over at Kris, who was reliving his fight for the fiftieth time, this time for a girl of about sixteen who looked worryingly impressed. Boys were so immature, I thought, even ones who'd seen the hard side. Would I ever find one I was happy with? I doubted it.

At the same time, there were quite a few good-looking boys at this party—most too old for me, but one or two . . .

Suddenly, quite to my surprise, I realized that Amelie wasn't the only one up for enjoying herself tonight. Maybe it was the pressure I'd been under, maybe the fear, but the thought of letting go felt like a lifeline. What a fantastic thing it was to dance, to socialize, to have fun! No one after you, no one hassling you, no one out to prevent you simply enjoying yourself!

What was I waiting for?

I put down my drink and was about to ask Amelie if she was dancing, when I realized she'd already gone. Through the misty lights and thumping beats I spotted her, throwing herself into the rhythm. Then, to my complete surprise, I caught sight of Kris dancing beside her, and my world was totally blown off its axis.

I don't know why, but I'd never imagined Kris dancing. He was so cool and self-contained, it was hard to imagine him losing himself to music. But here he was, in a kind of ecstasy, totally at the mercy of the beat, fired with the most amazing animal energy. Just as he'd got into one move, he went into another, then another, then another. I'd never seen anyone dance like it.

Amelie was obviously enjoying Kris's company on the dance floor. She started mimicking some of his moves, so he started making them more complicated, which made her laugh. Kris kept his eyes fixed on her, totally fearless despite the fact she was six years older and had a boyfriend at home.

The more I watched, the more I didn't like it, and the more I didn't like it, the more I realized the awful truth: *I* wanted to be dancing with Kris.

So I did. Not *with* him exactly, but as near as possible. I latched on to a couple of lads not much older than me, and started giving it everything I'd got. If Kris could surprise me, I thought, I could do the same to him.

The trouble was, Kris didn't react at all. Every time I caught his eye he ignored me. It was like I counted for nothing now he was with a real, grown-up woman.

Suddenly the music slowed. Kris was dancing really close to Amelie by now. He said something to her which I couldn't catch, then his arm went around her.

For a moment Amelie seemed to accept the situation. Then, gently but firmly, she removed his arm, said something with a laugh, and went off in search of other friends.

Ha! I thought. That's put a wrench in the works, mister! As if she's going to get off with a stupid kid like you!

And Kris did suddenly look very young and stupid. You could see the confidence drain out of him. He carried on dancing for a bit, then went off to get another drink. But five minutes later he was back, still ignoring me, with a new dancing partner, this time a girl about my age. She was obviously a lot easier to impress, and sure enough, after ten minutes or so, they sat down together.

I tried to ignore it, but next time I looked, they were snogging.

I felt gutted. Utterly gutted. More than that: I felt betrayed. In a strange kind of way, I did feel Kris was mine, that we were tied together, despite our differences. And anyway, I had much nicer legs than her, and it was a safe bet I was twice as brainy.

Still, I made sure no one saw what I was thinking. I danced harder than ever, threw my new locks around, chatted and laughed and even flirted. Right up to the time Kris stood up and made for the refreshments table.

Here was my chance to talk. I grabbed a cup and moved quickly. Despite the fact I was so upset with Kris,

I meant to be friendly, maybe swap a couple of witty comments, be like people are when they know there's a secret bond between them.

Then I saw a cigarette in his hand and my plans went right out of my head.

"What are you smoking for?" I said.

The moment I'd said it I knew I'd made a mistake.

"What are you?" said Kris. "My wife?"

For one scary moment that picture came into my mind. I pushed it quickly out again. "It's not clever or cool," I said.

"Who says I think it's clever or cool?" said Kris. "Maybe I just like it."

"You won't like it when you're lying in the hospital with your lungs rotting," I said.

"I can't afford the hospital," said Kris. He dipped a cup into the punch and swigged it down.

"There's alcohol in that," I said.

"There *is*?" said Kris. He dipped his cup in again.

"Don't!" I cried.

"What's it to you?" scoffed Kris.

"You'll talk too much," I said.

"I'm not an idiot," said Kris.

"You don't even know who she is," I said.

"Leave it alone, Jade, for God's sake!" said Kris.

My blood began to boil. "Do you know what really pisses me off?" I said.

"Ooo!" said Kris. "She swore!"

"You're sitting there snogging a total stranger," I said, "and when Mum died, and I wanted comfort, you couldn't even put your arm around me!"

Kris was unfazed, even though he could see I was about to cry. "You never asked," he said. With that, he turned on his heel, and I sank into a plastic chair, tears flowing.

This was the last thing I wanted. My fantastic new image, shattered. People asking me what was wrong, and me not even being able to answer. And meanwhile, through the mist of my tears, Kris with his face back on that girl's.

A woman I'd never met sat next to me. I started pouring my heart out to her, telling her I wanted Mum, telling her I never wanted to be in this situation, telling her how much I hated Kris and wished I'd never met him. Whoever she was, this woman was very patient and kind, and let me sob on her shoulder like an idiot. Then she found out someone to take me home, at which point Amelie arrived on the scene. She was upset I'd had such a bad time, but you could tell she didn't want to leave unless she had to. In the end Tom agreed to take me home, then go back for the others. I felt like a useless burden, but if I'd stayed I'd have been even more of one.

So much for my great night out.

Chapter Nineteen

Raff was ecstatic. "Mission accomplished!" he cried. He led the way to the living room, where Feela was licking herself furiously. She seemed hyper-alert, looking up and around with sudden, precise movements. But most importantly, she was safe and well.

"Where's Thumper?" I asked.

"Gone," said Raff. "We didn't want to tire the old boy out."

"Will she definitely be pregnant?" I asked.

"Oh yes," said Raff. "It's fail-safe with cats. See, the male has this barb—"

"Spare me the details," I said. I went down on to my knees besides Feela and stroked her head. She closed her eyes and relished my touch.

"Must be great being a cat," said Raff.

"What, getting all this attention?" I asked.

"Nice, simple relationships," replied Raff, and I had a feeling there was more he wanted to tell me. But right now it was hard enough coping with my own life.

"I wish I'd seen Thumper," I said.

"Believe me," said Raff, "you don't."

"Why?" I said. "Is he ugly?"

"He's had a hard life," replied Raff.

"I can't believe any cats are ugly," I said, running my fingers through Feela's lustrous fur.

"What about the ones the super-rich buy?" asked Raff. "You know, the ones with the flat faces."

"Who would want a cat with a flat face?" I asked.

"People with flat faces?" suggested Raff.

I laughed. After all Kris's games and put-downs, it was such a relief to be having a normal conversation with a man. Amelie was so lucky, I thought. Or maybe she was just the kind of woman who was attracted to nice, straightforward men. I always thought I'd be one of those, but obviously I wasn't, because I didn't fancy Raff one bit. No matter how much I fought it, I couldn't get the image of Kris dancing out of my head.

It was daybreak when the others got home. I heard them

making some food, laughing, and talking loud like drunk people do. Then there were some good-nights, followed by a creak at the lounge door. I peered from beneath my covers to see Kris's head poking around.

"How'd it go?" he asked.

"How did what go?" I replied.

"Feela!" he said.

"Oh," I replied. "Raff says she's pregnant."

Kris grinned broadly. "Can I come in a sec?" he asked.

"Go on," I said unenthusiastically.

Kris made a beeline for Feela, bent down and ruffled her neck. "Well done, you little tart," he said.

"Don't call her that!" I snapped.

"I'm only joking, for God's sake," said Kris.

"I don't find it funny," I replied.

"Give me a break," said Kris.

I watched Kris toying with Feela, and simmered. "Did you call that girl a tart as well?" I asked.

"What girl?" asked Kris.

"The one you were kissing," I replied.

Kris stood up. "Why are you acting like you're my girlfriend?" he asked.

I began to blush. "That'd be the day," I said.

"Yeah," said Kris. "It would."

"I don't see why people have to act like animals," I said.

"*What?*" said Kris.

"You heard me," I replied.

"We are animals," said Kris, changing tack.

"Don't be stupid," I replied.

"Look," said Kris, pointing at Feela. "Two ears, two eyes, nose, mouth, heart, lungs, liver . . . we're not that different."

"Feela can't choose what she does," I replied. "And anyway . . . we've got opposable thumbs."

"*What?*" said Kris.

"We've got opposable thumbs," I repeated. It was something I'd learned in biology which I'd never forgotten, for some reason.

"And . . . ?" said Kris.

"That's why we can write," I said. A little devil appeared on my shoulder, and I added, "Some of us."

Kris stared at me a long time. He wasn't enjoying sparring now. This fight was real. "God, I really enjoyed that party last night," he said.

I sat up, keeping my eyes fixed on Kris's leering face, ready to strike back at any moment. The time had come to unload all my suspicions.

"Why did you come with me?" I asked.

"You know why I came," he replied.

"I know what you told me," I said.

"That's enough then, isn't it?" said Kris.

"No, Kris," I replied. "It's not enough. Because I don't believe you. You're playing games with me all the time. For all I know this whole thing could be some stupid game you're playing."

"You're paranoid," said Kris.

"How come you knew about the raid?" I asked.

"I told you," said Kris. "I didn't know—I guessed."

"I don't believe you," I replied.

"What, do you think I'm working for Comprot?" asked Kris.

"You could be," I replied.

Kris just laughed.

"Look at all the information you're getting," I said.

Kris laughed again.

"You're using me somehow," I said.

Kris circled me slowly, then suddenly sprang forward.

"OK," he said. "You got me. Special Officer 265. Bio-terrorism Division."

"I'm not laughing," I replied.

"It's hopeless," said Kris. "I admit everything, and you

still don't believe me."

"You're right, it's hopeless," I replied.

"What are you going to do about it then?" asked Kris.

"I could go on alone," I replied.

"You reckon?" said Kris with a smirk.

"Yes," I replied. "I do."

"Suit yourself," said Kris. "I'll see Fay again then."

"Fay?" I scoffed. "That's her name, is it—Fay?"

"Ooh, Jade," said Kris. "You almost sound jealous."

"Kris, just shut up and get out," I snapped.

Kris stooped and ruffled Feela one more time. "Good-night, love of my life," he said. Then, just as he was leaving, he added, "And good-night to you too, Feela."

I sank back beneath the covers, upset and confused. Part of me really believed I should strike out on my own. Part of me sensed that this episode with Kris was just one chapter in a much longer story.

Chapter Twenty

The moment Amelie walked in I sensed something was wrong. She always seemed so unruffled, so sublime. But now she looked deadly worried.

"The group warning's gone out," she said.

"What happened?" asked Raff.

"They raided Frida," replied Amelie.

"Uh-oh," said Raff.

"Who's Frida?" I asked.

"She's our secretary," replied Amelie. "She's got the database. All our details are on it."

"How did that happen?" said Raff.

"Must have been someone at the party," replied Amelie.

I looked accusingly at Kris. Amelie laid a hand on my arm. "Sorry, lovely," she said. "You'll have to go."

"Group warning means we've got to clear away any evidence," explained Raff.

"You mean they could raid here?" I asked.

Raff nodded. The memory of being raided came back in every cruel detail. I did not want to go through that again.

"But will you still be able to take me?" I asked.

"*Us*," corrected Kris.

From Amelie's expression I immediately knew the answer.

"Doesn't matter," I said.

"I'm sorry, lovely," she replied. "Now they've got our details the first thing they'll check is the vehicle database."

"Can't we borrow someone else's van?" asked Kris.

"Everyone we know's on that list," replied Raff.

"We'll nick one," said Kris.

"No we won't," I replied.

"Why not?" said Kris. "We took the truck. We took the boat."

"That was different," I said.

"Forget it," said Amelie. "You won't get ten kilometers in a stolen vehicle."

Raff thought for a moment. "There is the skoot," he said.

"That's a point," said Amelie. "That's not registered."

"Can either of you ride a skoot?" asked Raff.

"I can," I replied.

Kris looked at me doubtfully.

"There was a track down the marina," I explained.

"Oh," said Kris. "*Daddy* bought you one."

"We hired it by the hour, actually," I replied.

Raff and Amelie weren't quite sure what to make of this conversation.

"Are you happy to ride it, Jade?" asked Amelie.

"Yeah, I'll do it," I replied.

"I reckon I can ride it, probably," said Kris.

I ignored him. "What about Feela?" I asked.

"There's a big pannier on the back," said Amelie. "Her box should go in OK."

"It's got holes so she can breathe," added Raff.

"Let's do it," I said.

The skoot was a lot bigger than the ones I was used to, but the controls all seemed to be the same. I just needed to give it a trial run—but first I had to get Kris off the front seat. He'd climbed aboard as soon as they'd brought it out, and was doing his best to look like he knew what he was doing.

"Throttle on the right hand?" he asked.

"That's it," said Raff.

"Gear-change on the left?" he asked.

"It's automatic," replied Amelie.

"All skoots are automatic," I added.

"Just testing you," said Kris.

Kris checked out a few more things, whistling as he did so. I'd never heard him whistle before, and it wasn't very tuneful.

"OK," said Kris. "I think I've got everything."

"Good," replied Amelie. "Hop off now so Jade can get the feel of it."

I was beginning to truly love Amelie. Kris, on the other hand, was going off her fast. But he did as he was told and I quickly took his place. The saddle felt familiar and comfortable, and I soon got used to the little differences from the skoots I'd ridden before. Raff fitted me with a helmet and I took the skoot for a spin around the block, steady and careful as always. Mum always said I was a natural rider, and with what lay ahead, I would need to be.

Feela put up the usual struggle against going into her box, but resigned herself pretty quickly to her fate, being dog tired after her wild night. Kris, on the other hand, did not intend to go so quietly onto the back seat.

"It's just going to look stupid!" he protested.

"Kris," said Amelie, "no one's going to know who you are, so what are you worried about?"

"*I* went on the back all the time," added Raff. "It was great."

"Yeah," said Amelie, "till you added the speed limiter."

"The override's just under the ignition, see?" said Raff.

"You never told me that!" said Amelie, and they launched into a mock fight, which broke the tension for a while—long enough for Kris to quietly slip into place and adopt as cool a pose as possible. Needless to say, he sat back and took hold of the handrails—he wasn't going to put his arms around me.

We checked the map and worked out the best route, avoiding all the main roads and the cameras. Amelie reckoned we could make Bluehaven within the day, even at the skoot's limited speed. My heart leaped at the thought, but after all that had happened, I wasn't taking anything for granted.

"Good luck, Jade," said Amelie. "We're all counting on you."

"Don't say that," I replied.

I tried to make the farewells as quick as possible. It was easier that way. But Raff, bless him, was such a touchy-feely person he just had to hug me and wish me the best. I think he might have tried to hug Kris as well if Kris hadn't deliberately looked the other way.

So there we were, back on the road, back to the world of endless uncertainty. But we weren't going far. After Kris had flapped his arm once or twice to indicate which way we should be going, I pulled into a side lane, took off my helmet, and motioned him to do the same.

"Listen, Kris," I said. "I'm under enough stress without you criticizing my driving. Either back off or get off."

"You're weaving about all over the place," said Kris.

"That's 'cause you're unbalancing me!" I cried.

"I'm too heavy to be on the back," said Kris.

I took a deep breath. "Listen," I said. "I don't have to go with you."

"You could have said that back at Amelie's," said Kris.

"I didn't want to have a row in front of them," I replied.

"Still think I'm working for the state?" sneered Kris.

I looked him in the eye. "Funny how they raided that secretary," I said.

Kris was unfazed. "If I'd given them a tip-off," he said, "they'd have raided Amelie's."

"Amelie didn't have the database," I replied.

"She had Feela," said Kris.

"Yeah," I said, "but they wouldn't get any more information once they'd got Feela, would they?"

Kris paused, weighing me up. "You should write books," he commented.

I said nothing. We stared at each other, not sure what to do next. Kris raised his eyebrows and smiled with one corner of his mouth. I briefly replayed Kris kissing that Fay, then pulled my helmet back on and restarted the skoot. We continued without another word, and Kris made no more hand signals.

Chapter Twenty-One

We made good progress down those back lanes. No cameras, not a lot of traffic, good weather, and no problems with the skoot. I was starting to feel confident, in control of my own destiny, a daughter Mum could be proud of. If it were possible, I'd have just kept riding, nonstop, all the way to Bluehaven. But we had to eat, check on Feela, and answer the calls of nature. Kris in particular needed to answer those calls. He'd drunk about a liter of orange juice before we left and his bladder was in danger of exploding.

Eventually we came across a picnic site which looked as if it could meet our needs. It was one of those sites which were off the road, down a lane—the kind of place which was often deserted. Often the automatic food-points were vandalized, and there was always the fear a gang of muggers might be waiting there. Somehow, though, I just didn't worry about those kind of things anymore.

It looked like we'd chosen the perfect place to stop. At the end of the lane was a wooded clearing without a soul in sight. The foodpoint had been demolished, but there were still a few picnic tables on the grass in front of a shallow artificial lake. Bushes and small trees were scattered around the area—apart from that, nothing but butterflies and dragonflies.

Kris pulled off his helmet and disappeared into the trees at the far side of the clearing. My first thought, however, was for Feela. As I opened her box, the poor thing refused to move a muscle. Despite the fact that she always struggled against going into her little jail, once she was used to it, she felt safer in than out. With some encouragement she did venture a quick glance over the top, but one crow's caw sent her cowering back down.

"Wish I could explain to you, Feela," I said, but all I could actually do was try to put an end to this journey as quickly as possible.

I closed Feela's lid, just to be on the safe side, and looked around for a suitable ladies' convenience. There was a row of thorn bushes, just head high, back to the left of the lane where we'd come in. I sauntered over to check it out, but as I did so, became aware of something black and metallic glinting behind it. At first I thought it might be some kind of litter skip—but the way it shone suggested it was too new for that.

I rounded the bushes and, to my horror, saw a giant motorbike. It was fitted with every gadget and gizmo you could imagine, and along the fuel tank was emblazoned the word COMPROT.

"Nice machine, eh?"

The voice seemed to come from nowhere. My heart leaped into my mouth as I turned to see a fully uniformed comper—black boots, black gauntlets, stunstem, billy club, spray, and gun. Fortunately, however, none of the weapons were in his hand, and on his face was a smile.

"Like it?" he asked.

"Very nice," I replied.

"Go on, hop on," he said. "I know you're dying to."

Was he playing a game with me? He didn't seem to be.

"I'll just look at it, thanks," I replied.

The comper gazed over at the skoot. "That your vehicle?" he asked.

"Yes," I answered nervously.

"You look a bit young to be riding a skoot," he observed.

"I'm sixteen," I replied.

"I believe you," he said with a wink. "Thousands wouldn't."

"How fast does your bike go?" I asked, quickly changing the subject.

"Two hundred, tops," he replied. "I take it easy, mind you. Never go over one-ninety."

I smiled weakly.

"Joke!" he exclaimed.

I smiled a little harder.

"Go on, get your leg over it!" he coaxed.

I decided it was easier to comply. It kept his attention off the skoot. With any luck he would soon get fed up with trying to impress me and go away.

"What d'you reckon?" he asked.

I didn't want to admit it, but after the old skoot, the Comprot bike felt fantastic. It was as if all the power of the state was concentrated into one supreme machine. How reassuring, I thought—provided you were on their side.

"Brilliant," I replied. "Thanks."

I began to dismount, and just as I did so, caught a glimpse of Kris emerging from the trees at the far side.

There was no way I could signal him to go back. He couldn't see me through the thorn bushes, and in any case, the comper would notice. I asked some stupid question about the brakes, just to keep the comper's attention away from Kris, but Kris, unfortunately, had seen him. Without thinking twice he headed towards us, planning to do what, I don't know. At any rate, the comper heard him coming.

"Oh," he said. "Didn't know you had a boyfriend."

Kris stopped, and tried to look vaguely threatening. At this point, the comper's manner changed. You could almost see the penny drop as he looked from one to the other of us.

"Let's take a look at this skoot, shall we?" he said, his voice no longer friendly.

The comper marched across the grass, casting a hostile look at Kris as he passed him. I hurried after him, hoping somehow to keep him away from the pannier, but Kris had other plans. He whipped the stun-stem from his inside pocket and ran full-tilt at the comper's back.

That comper must have had second sight. Before Kris could offer a single jab, he had whirled around, snatched the billy club from his belt, and smashed the stun-stem out of Kris's hand. Next second he was raining blows down on Kris, full force, dashing him to the ground then pummeling his defenseless body without mercy.

"Stop it!" I cried. "You'll kill him!"

The comper was deaf to my pleas. "Attack me, would you, punk?" he sneered, laying in now with his boots, which landed with sickening dull thuds on Kris's midriff.

I couldn't just stand there. Kris's stun-stem was still lying there on the ground, and almost before I knew it, it was in my hand. Within a few seconds I had switched it on and stabbed it into the comper's side. As he crashed to the ground I stabbed at him again and again till his spasms had stopped and he lay completely motionless.

"That's for Mum!" I cried. I felt a sob rising, but held it back.

Kris uncurled and raised himself painfully. "Good going, Ms. Pacifist," he grunted.

"I had to do something," I replied. My whole body was trembling now. I let the stun-stem drop from my hands.

Kris viewed the comper. "How many times did you use that thing?" he asked.

"I don't know," I said. "Lots."

"Jade, you're only supposed to use it once!" said Kris. He struggled to his feet, with a look of alarm on his face. "*Scheisse*," he said. "I think you've killed him."

"No I haven't!" I exclaimed.

Kris placed his finger against the comper's neck. "I can't feel a pulse," he said.

"Don't be stupid!" I cried. I got down myself and felt the hot, clammy neck, until at last I detected the faintest tremor. "There is a pulse!" I cried.

"I couldn't feel it," said Kris.

"You were pressing too hard," I replied. "He's alive."

Kris pondered for a moment. "Maybe it would be better if he was dead," he said.

"No, Kris," I replied.

Kris picked up the stun-stem and held it close to the comper's ear.

"No, Kris!" I yelled.

"Still think I'm working for Comprot?" asked Kris.

"No, I don't!" I cried. "Now leave him!"

Kris stayed motionless, stun-stem just centimeters from striking what would surely be a fatal blow.

"Don't play games with me!" I cried.

There was a pause, then Kris pocketed the stun-stem.

"With any luck he's brain-dead anyway," he said.

Kris helped himself to everything he could find on the comper's belt, then pulled the radio from the comper's pocket and smashed it to the ground. To complete matters he hobbled over to the bike, smashed the mirrors, and let down both tires.

"Come on," he said. "Let's get going."

Chapter Twenty-Two

I felt no guilt about what happened to that comper. My mind was totally focused on survival, and that meant counting down the signposts to Bluehaven, avoiding accidents, and most of all ensuring we didn't get caught. Despite the shock and the adrenaline I felt amazingly calm, almost robotic, my decisions clear and deliberate, my steering accurate, my control complete. Kris, like Feela, had accepted his fate as passenger now, and I was hardly aware he was there behind me. As soon as I stopped, however, I turned to see him as alive as ever.

"What have you stopped for?" he asked.

"Got to check on Feela," I replied.

"Why?" said Kris. "We stopped less than an hour ago."

"She's been in that box all day," I replied. "She hasn't eaten and she hasn't been to the toilet."

"If we keep going, we'll be there in two hours," said Kris impatiently.

I ignored him, climbed off, and began opening the box. Kris looked around anxiously. We were in a wayside beside some fields of sweetcorn with no houses or people in sight, but there was always the danger of a stray speed camera, even here—except I'd already checked that out.

Feela looked up at me and gave a low cry. I knew that cry well.

"She's got to pee," I said.

"We can't take her out here!" said Kris.

"There's a gate up ahead," I said, almost manically. "You get in the field and I'll lift her over the hedge to you."

Kris sighed. "Can't she wait?" he said.

"She's in pain!" I cried.

"I'll give her a Harpaxin," said Kris. "That'll put her out till we get there."

"She's pregnant, Kris!" I said.

"And?" said Kris.

"What's it going to do to the kittens?" I railed.

To my surprise, Kris didn't pursue the argument. Reluctantly, he climbed off the skoot, wincing as he did so.

"Are you all right?" I asked.

"Yes!" he snapped irritably.

Kris was lying, that was obvious. You could see by the way he was standing how much it hurt. As I observed him a switch seemed to be thrown in my mind and the violent, unreal scene came back full force. I saw the comper's body on the ground, my hand on the stunstem, Kris stopping me from almost certainly killing him. Reality hit home, the mask dropped and panic set in.

"This is a nightmare," I blurted.

"Cool it, Jade," said Kris.

"We've nearly killed a comper!" I cried. "What if they catch us? What'll they do?"

"They won't catch us," said Kris.

"They couldn't kill us, could they?" I blurted.

"They're not going to catch us!" repeated Kris.

"Kris, I'm scared!" I cried.

"Jade, you're panicking," snapped Kris.

"I know I'm panicking!" I cried. "I've got every bloody right to panic!"

"It's not going to help," said Kris.

"I can't help it!" I yelled, tears bubbling. "I'm scared! Don't you ever get scared?"

There was a long pause. "Just keep focusing on your mum," said Kris.

I calmed a little.

"Anger overcomes fear," declared Kris. "Like stone over scissors."

I calmed a little more. "Is that why you're a stone?" I asked.

"You're starting to suss me, Jade," replied Kris.

I considered him. "Where does it hurt?" I asked.

"Everywhere," he replied.

"Want me to kiss it better?" I said, trying to lighten the situation.

"Don't want poison in the wound," he replied.

"Suit yourself," I said curtly. Just as suddenly as I'd panicked, I was focused again. "Come on," I ordered. "Get in the field."

Just at this moment there was the sound of an engine—a hydro car. We both froze. Comprot used hydro cars. But this one turned out to be no more than a family cruiser, which passed us by with the usual odd looks, no more.

"This is too risky," said Kris.

I agreed. "Maybe the next village will have a toilet," I suggested.

"You're going to take Feela into a toilet?" said Kris.

"Why not?" I said. "At least it'll have a lock on the door."

Kris shrugged. "You know best," he said.

It was a long ride to the next village, which turned out to be one of the new inland marina towns, built around an artificial lake. It reminded me a bit of where I grew up, which was strange because it also felt totally alien and sinister, especially now it was growing dark. Everybody was a potential enemy now—the people loafing on their boats, the line in the deli, the parcel delivery men. Most of all, however, the cameras, because there were cameras everywhere. It was risky to stop here, but we had no idea how far the next village was, and the situation was getting desperate. As soon as I spotted a wash kiosk I pulled up. Kris climbed straight off the bike and began taking out Feela's box.

"What are you doing?" I asked.

"Taking her in," he replied.

"I'm taking her in!" I said.

"I'll be faster," said Kris.

"You won't know what to do with her!" I protested.

"I'll put her in the sink," said Kris. "Then if I go, she'll go."

It shocked me to hear Kris say this. It was one of Feela's weirdest habits, to wee in the bath when I was on the toilet. But Kris had never seen this—unless he'd been spying on me a lot more closely than I thought.

"How do you know she does that?" I asked.

"Lots of cats do it," replied Kris.

"How do you know?" I asked.

"For God's sake!" said Kris. "We ain't got time to stand around arguing!"

"You're right," I replied. "Wait here."

With that I seized Feela's box, dropped a coin into the slot, and walked into the kiosk. I wasn't sure how shocked Kris was about this as he still had his helmet on, but in any case the door soon closed and Feela and I had at least a few minutes' privacy.

The toilet kiosk was a dismal place, lit by a bright bluish light—just a toilet, a washbasin, and a white plastic floor which curled up to become white plastic walls. I took off my helmet, placed Feela's box on this floor, and opened the lid. She looked up at me with those beautiful black-rimmed eyes, just as cowed as before, even less willing to move.

"Come on, baby," I said, and lifted her gently from her prison. She didn't resist, but gave a meow of protest from her tense little body and began to scramble for freedom as I lowered her. She spilled over my arms on to the floor and immediately went into crouch position.

I knew Kris would be getting impatient outside, but I also knew Feela wouldn't be doing anything till she'd sounded out her new home. She tested her way around the small space, always nose first, paying particular attention to the toilet, before giving another, lower meow which I took as a sign to lift her into the sink. Immediately I sat myself on the toilet, and though we were in this strange alien pod, miles from home, the situation was familiar to Feela. She checked me out, looked about for potential enemies, and finally, thankfully, squatted herself down with her tail sticking backwards like a tail-gunner.

I don't know how long Feela had been saving this one up, but her personal jetstream seemed to last for at least a minute. The poor thing must have been in agony.

I flushed the toilet just to make Feela feel at home, lifted her out of the sink, and gave that a good flush as well. It certainly needed it.

"Sorry, babe," I said. "Back to jail."

Feela settled back into her box with a resignation which made me feel even more guilty.

"Promise you it won't be long now, babe," I assured her. And as I said it, I was overcome by a huge, unreasoning protective love. There would be no more fear now. There would be nothing but resolve.

Little did I know it, but I would soon be needing that resolve. Just as I exited the toilet, a group of three men were approaching Kris. They were an odd bunch—a tall, gangly youth, a balding older version of him in a garish purple tracksuit, and a squat little man with aggressive features like a pitbull terrier. I heard the balding man mutter "Go on then," and give the youth a little push in the back. The youth ambled reluctantly forward, glancing back over his shoulder as if for reassurance, only to hear the balding man bark, "Look like you mean business, son! Don't slouch!"

The youth reached us. There was a dull, defeated look on his face and really bad acne. "Can you take off your helmet, please," he said to Kris.

"Why?" said Kris.

This obviously threw the youth. He looked back again, only to see the balding man—presumably his dad—with arms folded, looking most unhelpful.

"Can you take your helmet off, please?" repeated the youth.

"I'm riding a bike!" sniffed Kris, with mild contempt.

The youth turned to the older men. "He says he's riding a bike!" he yelled.

The older men looked at each other and shook their heads. "Does he look like he's riding a bike?" said the squat man in a high grating voice, followed by a snigger.

"Please," pleaded the youth. "Take your helmet off."

By now, Kris was spoiling for a fight. "Who says?" he snapped.

"We're the Neighborhood Watch," said the youth.

"So?" said Kris.

"We're just making sure everyone follows the law," mumbled the youth apologetically.

"*Law?*" sneered Kris. "What law says I can't wear a helmet?"

The youth had no answer. "Dad," he called. "What law says he can't wear a helmet?"

"Local bylaw," replied the balding man.

"Local bylaw," repeated the youth.

I was starting to sense danger. I could see the older men were bristling for a fight with Kris. Sure enough, they marched forward, with an impatient huff at the hopeless youth. "Listen, son," they said to

Kris. "We've got a hotline to Comprot. Do you want us to use it?"

"I still don't see why I've got to take off my helmet," replied Kris.

The squat man moved in. "We're under instructions to check all strangers in the village," he croaked.

"Amber alert," added Baldy.

My sense of danger rose. The only amber alert I knew was a terrorist alert. Was it us they were calling terrorists?

"What's that about?" I asked, as coolly as possible.

"Never you mind," replied Baldy.

"They don't tell us," added the youth.

Baldy shot him the filthiest look imaginable.

"Well done, Evan," said the squat man sarcastically.

"Well they don't," mumbled the youth.

Baldy turned his attention back to Kris. "Ten seconds," he said. He took out his mobile.

"Go on, Kris," I said. This was no time for bloody-mindedness or stupid principles. They didn't seem to know who I was, so why should they recognized him?

Kris let the ten seconds tick away. But as Baldy made to tap his mobile, Kris slowly removed his helmet. Baldy gave a little smile of self-satisfaction, then concentrated his eyes. "Where'd you get those bruises?" he asked.

"I hit him," I replied.

The squat man gave a little snort of laughter. "Had a fight?" he asked.

"Caught him snogging another girl," I replied.

"Ha!" said the squat man. "Been a naughty boy, has he?"

Kris glanced at me out of the corner of his eye, then nodded.

"So what you doing here then, kids?" asked Baldy.

"Just passing through," said Kris.

"Stopped for the toilet," I added.

Baldy's attention turned to me. His eyes strayed down towards the box containing Feela. Without a second thought I grabbed at Kris's collar. "Is that lipstick?" I roared.

"Get off! No!" replied Kris, pulling away.

"It better not be, Kris, 'cause I don't wear lipstick!" I yelled.

"You're paranoid!" said Kris.

"Yeah, and you're a lying—"

"OK, OK, OK!" said Baldy. He moved in to keep the peace, forgetting all about Feela's box. "Get on your way now, kids."

"Better give them a pass, Osh," said the squat man.

"Oh yeah," replied Baldy. "They'll need one of them. Evan—got the passes?"

Evan, as usual, looked clueless. "Thought you'd got them, Dad," he said.

"Jesus Christ Almighty," said Baldy. "Can't you get *anything* right?"

Evan smiled weakly. Just for a second, he caught my eye. It was the briefest of glances, yet, strangely, it made a bond. We both thought the same of Evan's dad, that was clear.

"We'll just get on," I suggested.

"Oh no, no, no," replied Baldy. "If you don't get a pass from us, you'll get stopped by every watch in the county."

"There's some in the yacht club, Osh," said the squat man.

"Follow us, please," ordered Baldy.

We had little choice but to follow the three local heroes up the street, then through to the lake, where stood a typical modern yacht club, typical to me anyway, but totally strange to Kris. He parked up the skoot, which I'd quietly fitted with Feela's box, and we cautiously entered the building.

All my instincts were for safety. I quickly checked out

the area we'd walked into: toilets to the left, club office to the right, bar ahead. Front door the only available exit. The center smelled of stale beer and air freshener, and there were raucous shouts from the bar where a small crowd were watching a soccer match on a big screen.

Baldy ushered us into the office, but I made sure I stayed by the door. Evan hung around in the entrance area, between us and the exit, but he didn't pose much of a threat. We exchanged another quick glance, and I gave him half a smile.

Baldy was one of those people who liked to do everything slowly and properly, as slowly and properly as humanly possible. The passes weren't in their proper places, so he had to reorder them first. Then he had to find the right inkpad for his stamp and the right pen for his signature. Meanwhile it had gone strangely quiet in the bar. I assumed it must have been half-time in the match, till a bottle-blond woman marched in with a look of concern.

"You better come and have a look at this, Osh," she said.

Osh laid down his pen and followed her. We followed also, worried by the suspicious glances the woman had given us. There was dead silence in the bar, everyone focused on the screen. The soccer was gone and in its place was someone I recognized from the government. He was followed by shots of patients in a hospital somewhere in Asia.

I'd seen footage like this before. They were people with the human form of cat flu.

A news reporter came on. He was talking about a terrorist alert. A red alert.

Suddenly, dreadfully, I saw the motionless body of the comper we'd left at the picnic site. As he was lifted into an ambulance, a senior officer came on screen with a grave face.

I glanced at the exit doors. Evan was still guarding them.

The senior officer spoke direct to camera. "There is a high probability that the callous attack on officer Matthews was carried out by bioterrorists," he said. "We are seeking to interview two young people believed to be in possession of an illegal and probably diseased cat."

My blood froze. And then, to complete my horror, the next picture that appeared on the screen was of me.

Amazingly, no one connected the picture up onscreen with the girl standing at the door. Amelie had done a good job. But the moment Kris's picture came up, and it

171

was clear they were after a teenage couple, there was a single cry of "It's them!" followed by the most unearthly howl from the crowd. We bolted for the door, only to hear a cry of "Lock it, Evan!" from Evan's dad.

Everything that happened at this point seemed to occur in slow motion. Evan stood in front of us, one hand on the door. Our eyes met again, and I could see the fear in his. In that split second he had to make a decision, and it was a decision which, miraculously, went our way. He stepped aside, let us past and then, for good measure, closed the door. He must have locked it as well, because as we jumped on to the skoot there was a huge commotion inside the yacht club, and no one came out of it till I'd opened the throttle that sent the skoot leaping off down the road. A few tried to give chase but they had no hope of catching us, not on foot, anyway.

Once they got into their four by fours, however, it would be a different matter.

Chapter Twenty-Three

We'd hardly made a mile when the first one came up behind us. The lights reared up in my mirrors like pitiless eyes, blinding, full beam. I was already at top speed, riding for my life, and there was no way I could outrun it. Desperately I looked for an exit road, or even a way out over rough ground that a car couldn't follow. There was nothing. Then a shot rang out.

I looked around in terror. Kris was still hanging on, unhurt. But the four by four was skidding crazily across the road with a tire blown out.

Then I saw the gun in Kris's hand.

There was no time for questions. Kris must have taken the gun from that comper without me noticing, because if I had noticed, I'd have screamed bloody murder. Now, however, I was just grateful he'd saved us—till the next one came.

We made another mile or so without incident. Then a sound cut through the air like the howl of a devil—a Comprot siren. It was followed seconds later by a full-scale light-show in my mirrors—at least two sets of headlights and blue flashers to boot.

I glanced behind to see Kris reaching for the gun and furiously waved my hand for him to stop. If he tried to shoot out their tires we would get a lot worse in return. My frantic waving sent the skoot swerving over the road, and it took all my strength to pull it back in line. In any case Kris ignored me, only to find the gun had jammed. As he flung it pointlessly at our pursuers, I spotted a sign ahead and a turnoff. I had no idea where it went but I took it. As luck would have it, the road led into a forest of firs and ended in a row of barriers. On the other side of the barriers was a rough track.

The skoot was narrow enough to get between the barriers—just barely. We set off up the track as the sound-and-light show turned into the road behind us. I watched in my mirrors as the cars screched to a halt and compers piled out—armed to the teeth. Without a second thought I turned off the main track on to a cross track, crashing through a ditch and up into the woods.

Next second I was weaving a crazy pattern through the trees, as gun-lasers flickered behind and a volley of shots rang out. But there was no way they could see us now, and no way they could catch us either. I broke out of the trees on to another wide track, turned the throttle to max, and just kept riding till we could hear nothing of the compers nor see the tiniest flicker of their lasers.

Whatever we'd ridden into was a big place. Though it was clear we'd lost the compers, we were just as lost ourselves. It was almost as if we'd entered into some kind of Middle Earth, a place inhabited only by the things of nature, whose cries and scents filled our ears. I pulled up the skoot, climbed off, took off my helmet, and sank down on to my haunches, not knowing whether to laugh or cry. Moments later, Kris was beside me, also on his haunches and breathing heavily.

"You're a bloody maniac," he said.

"I'll take that as a compliment," I replied.

"It wasn't meant as one," said Kris.

"Leave off," I replied. "We're alive."

"Just about," said Kris.

I looked around. "I don't know where the hell we are," I said.

"It's OK," said Kris. "We're heading in the right direction."

"How do you know?" I asked.

"Last time we saw the sun," replied Kris, "we were heading towards it. That means we were going west. We never changed direction till we came off the road. That was a right turn. Next one was left. Then right. Then left again. So we're still heading west."

"Are you sure?" I asked.

"I've got a very good sense of direction," replied Kris.

The reality of what had just happened to us began to sink in. "They fired at us," I said.

"I noticed," replied Kris.

"Do you think it was real bullets?" I asked.

Kris gave a look of disbelief. "What do you think?" he scoffed.

"I don't know!" I snapped. "It might have been that stuff they use on demos!"

"Jade," said Kris. "We're terrorists. They don't use dumshot on terrorists."

"*I'm* not a terrorist!" I cried.

"Try telling them that," replied Kris.

"You shouldn't have used that gun," I said.

"For Christ's sake!" cried Kris. "I saved us!"

"You've upped the stakes," I replied.

"Jade," said Kris, "there's a red alert. You can't up the

stakes from a red alert. The only reason they issue a red alert is to give them the right to shoot on sight."

Shoot on sight. The words themselves hit me like bullets. No questions. No doubts. We were no better than animals now.

"I need to rest," I said.

"No time to rest," replied Kris.

"Kris, I'm exhausted!" I cried.

"*They're* not resting!" snapped Kris. "They're cutting off the exits as we speak."

"But this place is massive," I protested.

Kris looked around. The dark shadow of a hill rose doomily ahead of us. "Let's climb that," he said. "Then we'll see the lay of the land."

"And they'll see us," I replied.

"We've got to take that risk," said Kris.

"What about Feela?" I asked.

"We'll have to leave her here," replied Kris.

"I'm not leaving her!" I cried.

"It'll take twice as long with her," said Kris. "And if we do get spotted, we'll have to move fast."

"Why don't you just go up?" I asked.

"We can't risk getting split," replied Kris. As he said this, his eyes gave a side-to-side flicker, and I guessed there was another reason. Whether it was through fear, common sense, or some secret affection, he didn't want to be apart from me. "We can be up and back in fifteen minutes," he added.

I opened Feela's box. She crouched nervously in the corner, looking up at me with those timeless eyes, irresistible. I stroked her head, flattening her ears and covering her eyes as her mother's tongue must have done once. As always, she accepted my service with patience, but she stayed rigid and produced no purr. I put a little food in with her, closed the box, and reluctantly pushed the skoot under the cover of some trees.

"Let's be quick then," I said.

Worn footsteps on the hill showed that we weren't the first to climb it. We were glad of those footsteps because the hill was steep, very steep. I kept my eyes fixed on the crest, but the crest seemed to keep receding, maybe because the angle of the hill was changing. The higher we got, the more scenery we could see—dramatic wooded hills and secret glades, here and there an outcrop of rock, all sheltered beneath a sky which seemed to have a thousand more stars than we saw in town.

Finally, however, we reached a kind of pinnacle, from

which there was a short, jagged walk to another slightly higher peak, this one surrounded by what looked like ancient earthworks—a moat, maybe, now swallowed by grass. We made our way over to this final peak, and as we reached its summit, a fantastic vista opened up before us. To my amazement, we were overlooking a huge river delta, sweeping down to the open sea. The harbor, the lights, the ferries, and the big hotels indicated it could only be one place: Bluehaven.

"We're there!" I gasped.

"It's farther than it looks," said Kris.

We sat on two rocks and considered the options. "We're going to need help," I said.

"What kind of help?" asked Kris.

"Help getting a boat, for a start," I said.

"How are we going to get that?" asked Kris.

"Amelie?" I suggested.

"We can't risk texting her," said Kris. "They'll get a fix on us."

"But Comprot know we're here anyway," I pointed out. "And by the time they home in on us, we'll have moved."

Kris wasn't convinced. "We don't want to give them anything," he said. "It's going to be hard enough as it is."

I pondered. "We should have brought Feela up here," I said. "Then we could just carry on on foot."

"You've changed your tune," said Kris.

"I didn't realize it was so close," I replied.

"Let's go back and get her now," said Kris. "While we've still got the cover of darkness."

Kris had spoken too soon. At that very moment, a pair of spotlights appeared over the horizon, beaming down on the hills to our left.

"Chopper!" cried Kris.

There was no time to get back down the hill. We dashed for the grassy moat around the hilltop and tucked ourselves under some overhanging boulders. Without pause for thought, Kris pulled me tight beside him. I could smell the musty scent of his hair and feel the warmth of his breath on my hand. Kris's breath was coming short and fast, and so was mine. That wasn't surprising—considering the danger we were in.

Suddenly the area around us was lit by a brilliant light. Every blade of grass and tuft of heather was picked out in glorious color. Kris gave a sudden tug on my arm to pull my elbow closer. Then, thankfully, the light passed and we breathed again.

"Let's move," said Kris.

We scrambled out of our hidey-hole and raced down the mountain, the sharp angle making downward flight dangerous and difficult. Short fast skidding steps, heels digging in as a brake murdered my calf muscles and made my lungs as sore. Only when I reached the bottom did I dare to look back to see those sinister lights still scanning the hills.

It was as well we'd hidden the skoot. The woods gave us good cover. My first thought, as ever, was for Feela, and when I'd checked she was still there and still alive we planned our next move.

"We'd better get deeper into this wood," I said.

Kris was reluctant. "Let's see if they go away," he said.

"I'm not going on now," I said.

"So where are you going?" asked Kris.

"Just somewhere sheltered," I replied. "Somewhere we can lie down for a while."

Kris studied me. He could see my tiredness, and also my determination. In him, I could see the usual animal intelligence at work, but also something new—something like consideration. "OK," he said. "Let's gather our strength. We'll need it tomorrow."

Chapter Twenty-Four

Not far into the wood we began to hear running water. Instinctively we moved towards it. Our supplies were low and running water was safer to drink than still water. That was the reason Feela had her curious habit of licking at the cold tap until I turned it on, then lapping the thin stream of water, sometimes for minutes, rather than drinking from a bowl or a puddle.

The path was getting more difficult. We made the decision to dump the skoot. There was no way we could ride it over the rough terrain between the mountain and Bluehaven anyway. Kris took Feela's box and we made our way down a winding path to where the sound of water was very loud indeed.

We soon found out why. It was more than a stream that awaited us. We emerged into a dell beside a wide pool, into which poured a high, narrow waterfall. Above that, more pools and waterfalls, scattered randomly among the rocks. Above that, yet more pools, and a great fall high above us, like the lip of a giant cup emptying its contents in a smooth milky film, glimmering in the moonlight.

"Let's stop here," I said.

Kris's calculating eyes ran all over the area. Only one way in and one way out. A flat bed of rock to lie on, and if we got tight to the edge nearest the trees, complete cover.

"OK," he replied.

It almost seemed as if nature had found us a home. Kris took out the sleepbag he kept in his backpack and laid it on the ground, while I sorted out the small amount of food we had left and filled a plastic bottle from the pool. Once we were settled, I opened Feela's box and began the slow, difficult task of coaxing her out. Her beautiful, profound eyes peered out at the strange surroundings and her ears flattened back at the sound of the water. Eventually, however, I persuaded her to climb tentatively out of her prison and crouch warily beside me. Low to the ground, eyes and ears flickering to every new sight and sound, she crept about a meter one way, then the other, always checking back to where she started and the perilous safety it afforded.

How alike we were now.

"It's OK, beautiful," I said. "You're OK."

I ran the back of my finger along her head and down between her tiny shoulder blades. She gave out a little purr, which was so reassuring it could have been a choir of heavenly angels singing the "Hallelujah Chorus."

"She's where she should be now," I said. "In nature."

"Give over," said Kris. "Cats have lived in houses since the Egyptians."

"How come you know so much about cats?" I asked.

"You asked me that before," replied Kris.

"And what did you say?" I asked.

"Research," replied Kris.

"Research," I repeated.

"If I like something," added Kris, "I find out about it."

I studied Kris's eyes. "Why have you got yourself in this situation?" I asked.

"Don't start that again," replied Kris.

"I'm not being suspicious," I said. "I just want to know."

"Why?" said Kris.

I put a hand to my head. "Kris, don't mess with my

head!" I cried. "They could kill us tomorrow! I just want to understand you!"

Kris said nothing.

"I *had* to save Feela," I said. "You had a choice."

"Not really," said Kris.

"What do you mean, not really?" I asked.

Kris picked up a stone and lazily lobbed it into the pool. I kept my eyes fixed on the side of his face, until suddenly he turned, fixed his steel-blue eyes on mine, and said, "Jade. There's something you ought to know."

"What?" I asked, fearfully.

"Feela's my cat," replied Kris.

"What do you mean?" I asked.

"I mean," said Kris, "I liberated her."

"Liberated her?" I repeated. "What from?"

"The breeding center," replied Kris.

I gazed at Kris's impassive eyes in disbelief. Suddenly everything made sense: the power he had over Feela, the details he knew about her, the readiness with which he'd thrown in his lot with me. "And you put her in my garden?" I said.

"She went missing when I lived on Chapel Street," said Kris. "You found her."

"Then . . . why didn't you tell me she was yours?" I asked.

"I didn't want her back," said Kris. "She was safer with you."

"You could have told me!" I cried.

"You wouldn't have kept her!" cried Kris. "And besides . . ."

"What?"

The trace of a smile came on to Kris's lips. "I wanted the scales to fall off your eyes," he said.

"What does that mean?" I asked.

"Face it, Jade," said Kris. "You were a sucker."

"I was not!" I protested.

"You believed everything you were told," said Kris. "You trusted everyone but me."

"That's not true," I said.

"But now," continued Kris, "you understand me." As if to prove his ownership of Feela, he clucked, she went over to him, and he softly rubbed the base of her spine. She lowered her front end to the ground and put her tail to one side.

"So you're happy now, are you?" I said.

"In a way," he replied.

"Now my mum's dead," I continued.

"I never knew that would happen," he replied.

"No," I said. "But when it did, you might have put an

arm around me."

The thought of these events broke down the wall I'd determinedly built around myself, and I began to cry again. Almost immediately, completely to my surprise, I felt Kris's arm around my shoulder. Instinctively I leaned my head against his chest, and a few moments later he began to stroke my hair—tentatively at first, then with the same sure touch he showed with Feela. I raised my arm, grasped his shoulder, and let the sobs overtake me. When they finally subsided, we just stayed as we were. Feela nudged at my leg, anxious to get in on the act. It was as if she sensed we were a pride now, a family, and our place was all together.

That was exactly how it felt to me. All the talk and the game-playing meant nothing once we were in contact. Quite simply, it was right.

Neither of us wanted to speak. We sat in silence for an age, Kris gently whisking a tuft of my hair, me tickling Feela's chin. A fantastic feeling of strength had come over me, like the two of us together were this massive force for good, a force that could change the world.

"Supposed to be good to cry," said Kris finally.

"Haven't you ever cried?" I asked.

"Course I have," he replied.

"When was the last time?" I asked.

"Not sure," replied Kris. "I think it was when they took away my pacifier."

I laughed. "You'll get cancer if you block up your feelings," I said.

"Oh yeah?" said Kris. "Sure it ain't cat flu?"

"It's true!" I said. Kris didn't bother to argue, which troubled me slightly, because I was only repeating something I'd heard.

"So do you feel better now?" asked Kris.

I craned my neck upwards and looked at him. "What, from crying?" I asked.

Kris nodded. He looked so different now. Open. Curious.

"Actually," I said, "I feel sick."

"That's a shame," said Kris.

I gave him a playful slap. "Yeah," I said. "'Specially if I'm sick over you."

Our eyes were locked together, challenging each other—to what, I didn't know. But Kris seemed to. He brought his mouth to mine to kiss me. I didn't respond.

"What's the problem?" he said.

"I'm too tired to get involved in something I don't

understand," I replied.

Kris laughed. "You're funny," he said.

"I must be," I said, "to like you."

"Oh, you *do* like me then," said Kris.

"Course I do," I replied.

"Always thought so," said Kris, grinning.

"Typical egotistical boy," I replied.

"I don't think you could ever call me typical," said Kris.

This time I didn't argue. I rested my head right up against his chest, feeling his skinny ribs rise and fall. No matter how forceful his personality, his body was as fragile as Feela's. The thought of those armed men, and the bullets they wanted to put into him, made me both terrified and raging angry. I thought again of the phrase that had come to me as I'd remembered Mum: *let your escape be my memorial.* And I knew that whatever the next day would bring, my resolve would be total, because now I was fighting to save two beings I loved.

Chapter Twenty-Five

I slept lightly, in fits and starts, but even in my dreamworld monsters surrounded us, and Feela was in constant danger of being snatched, or shot, or crushed beneath the pitiless wheels of a Comprot truck. Each time I woke I reached straight out for her, feeling such immense relief as my hand hit on her warm fur—except just after dawn had broken, when I felt nothing but cold rock, then saw to my relief that she'd moved to take advantage of Kris's cozy back.

Kris, miraculously, was sound asleep. I ran my hand over the top of his shorn head, flattening the soft bristles one way, then the other. For once he was helpless. I had total power over him, and I had to admit I liked the feeling. I stayed there, unmoving, for an age, my eyes roving around the stones that littered the area. Most were large, pale pebbles, but here and there one was broken, revealing a dark inner with razor-sharp edges. Dimly I remembered our history lessons at school, and how fascinated I'd been by the Stone Age and the flint tools people once fashioned. If this was flint, I thought, maybe I could make an axe with it, and it would have some mystic power, and . . .

Yeah, right.

Anyway, nature was calling. I slipped off through the wet, dewy bracken to find a private space to do a wee. To my amazement, Feela came after me, hoping, maybe, I might lead her to a place of greater safety. If only.

As I squatted there, Feela arched herself against my knee, just as she'd always done in the toilet at home: head-flank-tail, head-flank-tail in little circuits of delight. To her it was just another day. Just then, however, a wood pigeon flew up from the tree in an almighty clatter, and Feela dropped instantly into a crouch, ears pricked, eyes scanning manically. Then the fear passed, and she went back on another circuit.

How I envied her. Fear was a momentary thing for her. She couldn't imagine the day ahead or ponder the day before. She couldn't spend weeks on end panicking about an exam, or endlessly reliving the moment she saw her mother dead. She didn't hear the distant noise of a chopper and imagine the compers in full armor, training the sights of their guns on us. Then again, she couldn't plan for the danger ahead, or work out a way—any way—past it.

I returned to Kris and knelt down beside him. As I did, his eyes opened. "I'm cold," he said.

Instinctively I pulled him towards me, and he put up no more resistance than Feela. I held his head against my chest, reversing roles from the night before. The sun was up now, although it was invisible behind a sheet of milky cloud. But still the morning was beautiful, and the steady cascade of water into the waiting pools illustrated the loveliness of life with an intensity which was almost cruel.

Kris caught sight of Feela, reached out, and tickled her chin.

"All right, beautiful?" he said.

"Fine thanks," I replied.

"Good," said Kris.

There was a short silence.

"It's quiet," I said. "They must have given up."

"Actually," replied Kris, "they came over three times in the night."

"You were awake?" I asked.

"I always sleep with one eye open," said Kris.

I smiled to myself, having watched him out cold just five minutes before. How he loved to romanticize himself.

"So what would you normally be doing at home, this time in the morning?" I asked.

"This and that," replied Kris.

"I'd steer clear of 'that' if I were you," I said.

"I'll stick to 'this' then," replied Kris.

"Yes," I said. "You stick to 'this.'"

Unable to prevent myself, I bent down and gave him a little kiss on the mouth. Instantly an animal urgency came into his eyes, and he grabbed the back of my neck. I pulled away quickly.

"Come on," I said. "We've got to go."

Kris gazed at me with level eyes, unimpressed. "You want to get your head sorted out," he said.

"Whatever," I said.

"*Whatever*," he mimicked.

I filled a water bottle from the nearby pool while Kris fed Feela some dried food then put a small bag of it in my jacket pocket for later in the day. Breakfast for us was a few biscuits and a banana, then everything was packed, including Feela, who offered more resistance than she'd done since we left Amelie's. As we set off she was mewing loudly—not that it mattered, because no one was going to hear her.

We navigated by the big hill we'd climbed the night before. We knew if we went around it we'd be heading for Bluehaven, but we had to do this without coming into the open. So we stayed on the fringe of the forest, under cover but still in sight of the hill. We walked on a soft carpet of dry pine needles, saying nothing but what needed to be said, moving purposefully, efficiently, quickly. Feela settled back into silence, and for a long while we heard nothing but birds.

The farther we progressed without coming across any sign of Comprot, the more optimistic I became. It was, after all, a big, big area, and even if there were hundreds of compers, they couldn't cover all of it and Bluehaven as well. At the same time, however, the woods weren't half as wild as they looked. Well-worn paths crisscrossed them at regular intervals, and every minor crossroads meant an anxious, hasty glance in at least three directions.

Finally our luck ran out. A bubble of human voices suddenly competed with the birdsong. They weren't far away and they were getting closer.

Kris and I stood absolutely still, as still as Feela stalking a bird, senses working overtime. If we tried to move away from the voices, their owners might hear our footsteps, and in any case, we were as likely to run into them as to get away.

A twig cracked. The volume of the voices rose sharply. They were right on the path in front of us!

Instantly we dove for cover. Fortunately for us, there was a great mound of dead pine needles close by, at least two meters wide by a meter high. Behind that the ground dipped into a small hollow, so that we were just about obscured from view. I pulled Feela's box tight towards me and concentrated on breathing in silent, shallow drafts.

They were near, desperately near. I pressed in closer to the mound of pine needles, but at that moment made a shocking discovery.

The mound was alive.

Before my horrified eyes, a boiling mass of giant ants with red bellies and black heads was swarming over the pile of pine needles, infesting every centimeter with sinister action. One gang was dragging a helpless beetle to its doom, while others fought, greeted, carried, and rearranged in sudden definite spurts, ruthlessly purposeful.

I gritted my teeth and fought my instinct to cry out. The brutal little creatures were over me, over Kris, over Feela's box. But their monstrous nest was all that protected us from whoever was on the path.

By now, the voices were loud enough to hear:

"How many do you reckon then?" said a female voice.

"According to the media, could be thousands," replied a male voice.

"That comper weren't saying much," said the woman.

"Well, he wouldn't, would he?" replied the man.

The couple moved past and their conversation became a distant babble. I leapt up and began furiously brushing ants from my legs. "What are they?" I hissed.

"Formica," whispered Kris. "Wood ants."

"They're disgusting!" I hissed.

"They're survivors," replied Kris. Obviously he felt a kinship with the ants, but I felt the opposite. With their black, glinting, helmeted heads they were like an army of miniature compers. It was the beetle I identified with—the outsider they were programmed to destroy.

The image of that ant nest stayed with me as we pressed on through the forest. I thought of the compers we'd known at home, the friendly neighborhood ones who asked after Mum's health, and I wondered if they'd be amongst that army the passersby had been describing. I fantasized seeing them amongst the marksmen, calling out to them, having them save us. But deep down I knew this was nonsense. No matter how normal and human they'd seemed at our doorstep, they were the enemy now, and their private sympathies would count for nothing.

I began to sense that civilization was near—or what I used to think was civilization. The hill had all but disappeared behind us and the noise of traffic was growing. We came on a big wide path with worn tire tracks on either side—obviously a main thoroughfare through the forest. After a short debate, we agreed to head alongside this path, still under cover of the trees, so we could get a better idea of what was awaiting us at the edge of Bluehaven.

We found out soon enough. The meeting of the path and the road was festooned with compers. Everyone traveling down the road was passing through a checkpoint—some allowed through, some greeted with suspicion and stopped. As we watched from our hidey-hole, a group of young people were ordered out of their minibus and searched. Why, we had no idea. None of them looked like us.

"The roads are out, then," I whispered.

"We knew that anyway," replied Kris.

We pondered the alternatives. There was no point in heading back—Comprot would be covering every route out of the forest. There was no way forward—the forest ended at the road ahead. That only left sideways, skirting the trees till we found a weak link in the Comprot lines —if such a thing existed. But it was hard to believe there was a road or path out of here which they wouldn't have covered.

We hadn't moved far when our hopes received another blow. This side of the forest was bordered by a high metal fence, on the other side of which was some kind of park. The fence was a good three meters high and topped by razor wire. Kris gazed upwards and shook his head.

"I've tried to climb one of those before," he said.

"And?" I said.

He pulled up his trouser leg to show an ugly scar which ran the length of his inside calf.

"Nice," I said.

"I work out," quipped Kris.

"The scar, I meant," I replied. It was funny how we could joke in this situation, but it seemed to come naturally. I think they call it gallows humor.

"We could always cut through it," I suggested.

"Yeah," said Kris. "As long as you brought the oxyacetylene torch."

Kris continued to gaze at the top of the fence, but my eyes had turned to the ground. Some ingenious creature had found its own way past the fence by burrowing beneath it.

"Look," I said. "That's what we need to be—a rabbit."

Kris followed my gaze. "Badger," he corrected.

Suddenly a lightbulb went on. "Why can't we?" I said.

"What with?" said Kris. "That ground's bone hard."

I looked around. There were a few broken branches, but they were far too soft and bendy for digging. Other than that, just some large round rocks, like the ones at the waterfall.

Of course! Stone Age tools!

I picked up the nearest rock and dashed it with all my strength on to another stone. The rock cleaved neatly into three, each with hard, sharp edges. Before Kris's amazed eyes, I began chipping the pieces against each other, making my own crude version of a Stone Age axe.

"Come on," I said. "You do the same."

Without a word Kris picked up a second piece and began hammering it against one of the bigger stones. In a few minutes we had a pair of digging tools—pathetic compared to what ancient man (and woman) made, but good enough to loosen the earth around the badger's hole. Our hands could do the rest.

The job was easier than I expected. Beneath the hard surface the ground was relatively crumbly, and soon Kris's skinny body was testing out the depth of our burrow. After a little more frantic digging and scooping, he'd inched himself under the fence and emerged, filthy and triumphant, the other side. I pushed through Feela's box and the bags, then did my own scrabbling limbo dance through to the rough grass boundary of a gigantic corrugated iron shed, to the right of which was an equally gigantic concrete yard. To the right of that was another fence and beyond that another yard and buildings.

We did a quick recon. There didn't appear to be anyone around. At first we thought it was because the place was disused then it suddenly occurred to me, for the first time, that it was Sunday. Since we'd started our journey all the hours and days had run into one.

As we set off up the yard, with no view of what lay at the end of it, it became clear that the huge building next to us was some kind of factory. Farther up the yard were monstrous sheets of rusting metal, stacked in neat and meaningless piles next to an equally rusty railway line. We walked silently through this bleak and alien place, as if in a dream, wondering where it would ever end. But the piles only led to more piles, until I wondered if we would ever escape this cold, dead, heavy metal hell. Finally, however, there was another fence, not such a tall one, with no razor wire.

On the other side of that were cars.

Cars, as far as the eye could see.

We hadn't reached the road, however. The cars, like the sheets of metal, were arranged in military lines, empty of drivers and completely motionless. With the aid of some pallets, Kris climbed over the fence, and I handed him Feela, then made my own way over. Again, there was no sign of life in the yard, nothing but the idle machines workers had wasted their time making. The fact there wasn't a cloud in the sky or a breath of wind only added to the sense of unreality.

"What are they all doing here?" I asked.

"Rusting," said Kris.

"But there's thousands!" I said.

"This whole plant must have gone bust in the last crash," said Kris.

"Why don't they just give the cars away?" I asked.

"What?" said Kris. "And drive down prices? You'll be suggesting they give away cats next."

We fell back into silence. It didn't pay to get carried

away in conversation when a helicopter could appear at any second. I'd seen enough *Crimewatch* episodes to know how fast they could arrive, how far they could see, and how accurately they could shoot. It was strange to remember how reassuring that had once seemed.

Half hypnotized by the vast army of cars, it almost came as a surprise to see an end to it. But finally we glimpsed a fence ahead. As we drew closer to this our hearts sank. It was just the same as the fence we'd first burrowed under, but without a helpful patch of earth below—just rock-hard concrete.

Soon it became apparent there was only one way out of the car graveyard: a fortified gate a hundred meters to our left. Overlooking this gate was a gatehouse, and inside this gatehouse was a security guard.

"Maybe we could overpower him," suggested Kris.

"No way," I said.

"Why not?" said Kris. "There's two of us."

"He could be armed," I replied.

"Security guards can't carry guns," said Kris.

"No," I replied. "But they carry everything else."

Kris weighed up the options. "Got any better ideas?" he asked.

"Create a diversion," I suggested.

"How are we going to do that?" asked Kris. A few days ago he would have said this scornfully. Now it was just a question.

"How far can you chuck a stone?" I asked.

Kris was straight on to my wavelength. Not far away the concrete surface was cracked, and with a little effort he was able to pry out a decent-sized rock.

"If he comes out," said Kris, "get ready to run like hell."

Kris drew back his arm and flung the rock for all he was worth. It landed with a satisfying thud on the cars beyond the gatehouse. Sure enough, the guard was out like a darting fish. His eyes were locked on to the area where the rock landed, but to our intense frustration he moved no farther than the gate.

Kris yanked up another rock.

"No!" I hissed. "He'll see where it came from!"

The security guard was still scanning the far side of the yard. He lifted a phone to his lips.

"Shit," murmured Kris.

"Listen," I whispered. "What if we split up . . . then you attract his attention—he's bound to chase you. Then I'll get in the gatehouse and open the gate."

"You'll have to take Feela," said Kris.

"Of course," I replied.

A flash of doubt crossed Kris's face.

"You'll skin him, no worries," I said.

Kris's mouth smiled, if not his eyes. "Course," he said. "You ready?"

"Ready," I replied.

Kris slipped off between the cars while I made my way closer to the gate, keeping as low and silent as a huntress. The security guard was still on the phone, to whom was anybody's guess. But his head shot up at a yell of "Hey!" and the sight of Kris standing on the roof of a car, doing a little shimmy for good measure.

I could have done without the amateur dramatics. There was no point in winding the guard up as well as attracting his attention. But that was Kris and, most importantly, his performance worked. The security guard marched purposefully towards him, leaving the gatehouse unguarded. I raced towards it for all I was worth, threw open the door and found myself face to face with a picture of the comper we'd had the fight with on the front page of the *Daily People*, under a headline saying "FIND THE MONSTERS THAT DID THIS."

I ripped the paper from the desk and to my relief found the gate controls beneath it. I stabbed the open button, the gate began to rise, and I fled back outside. It was only now, to my horror, that I saw the security guard bearing down on me full-tilt.

I ducked beneath the gate and ran, but Feela's box weighed me down and unbalanced me. The guard was gaining by the second, his heavy footfalls hammering the pavement behind me. I chanced a desperate look behind to see, to my fantastic relief, the guard crashing forward to the ground, rugby-tackled with immaculate skill by Kris. Such was the force with which he crashed to earth, the guard was too shocked and winded to rise again, and Kris and I made our hectic escape around the silent and deserted streets of the industrial park until the car graveyard was well out of sight and we could pause to recover.

Even in this desperate state, panting for breath, Kris felt the need to explain to me the excellence of his technique and the importance of getting your man around the knees. But my ears were attuned to something other than the sound of Kris's prattle.

"Can you hear . . . *drums*?" I asked.

Kris listened. "Yeah," he said. "I can."

The day was so unreal by now, the unexpected seemed almost normal. We set off again, walking briskly, casting anxious glances both behind and ahead. The noise of the drums seemed to rise up and fall back again, eventually becoming completely drowned by the noise of traffic. We were approaching a main road, maybe *the* main road into Bluehaven.

Our first sight of this road was not encouraging. The first vehicle to pass was a Comprot armed response unit. We ducked back behind a hedge, thankful the van had been going far too fast to notice us. To our dismay, however, the armed response unit was quickly followed by a Comprot mobile video unit, a Comprot special tactics unit, three mobile detention units and at least eight more Comprot vans, each loaded to the brim with fully tooled-up compers.

"Talk about overkill," whispered Kris.

"That can't be all for us," I whispered back.

Just as I said this there was a breath of wind, and the sound of drums once more rose up. But this time, there was more. Voices. Many voices. And as we crouched in fear of our lives, these voices grew and grew until we could make out the actual words they were chanting.

The words they were chanting were our names.

"It's a lynch mob!" I hissed.

Kris said nothing, but we both knew our chances were

close to zero with the whole town mobilized against us. If the worst came to the worst, could we expect the compers to protect us from a crowd fired up by all the news stories? And what would they do to Feela?

For a second it crossed my mind to just open the basket and let Feela go. At least then she'd have a fighting chance—or a better chance than us, at any rate.

"We've got to go back," said Kris.

"Kris, we can't go back!" I hissed.

"We're gonna get seen," said Kris.

"If we move they're even more likely to see us," I replied.

The drums were now thundering with a murderous intensity, echoing the rhythm of the savage chants. Soon it was too late to do anything other than sit tight and pray no one took a detour around the corner of our side road. Through the thin defense of the hedge we saw two lines of grim-faced compers, on foot this time, coming up the pavement either side of the road.

The noise of the mob was now deafening. Suddenly they came into view, fists pumping and faces ablaze. The front line held a banner as wide as the road, and on this banner were the words FREE CATS LEAGUE.

My eyes met Kris's, both of us realizing the astonishing

truth that this fearsome crowd was not out to kill us, but to defend us.

Suddenly our hopes rose again. Big crowds meant chaos. We could lose ourselves in a big crowd.

Yes! That was it!

"Kris!" I urged. "Let's get in with them!"

"That's mad," replied Kris.

"No it isn't!" I whispered. "They'll never see us in the middle of that lot!"

Kris considered.

"Jade, it's a big risk," he said.

"Maybe Amelie's there," I suggested.

Kris's expression changed. Suddenly, it seemed, he could see the sense in my suggestion. I felt relieved that I'd won him over but at the same time the old pangs of jealousy came back, stronger than ever.

"Look," said Kris, grabbing my arm. "Here's our chance."

Out on the road a confrontation was taking place. A gang of compers had surrounded a protester and were insisting she took her mask off. Other protesters were getting involved in the row, the march had broken into random groups, and the lines of compers had broken as well. With no time for hesitation, we leapt from our hiding place and within a few moments had buried ourselves in the heart of the crowd.

The confrontation ended, the march came back together again and moved off. The compers hadn't spotted us, but it wasn't long before the people around us had. We urged them quickly to hush and not give the game away. One quick-thinking individual offered to change jackets with Kris, while another lowered their flag to hide Feela's basket. As the drumming and chanting rose up again the sense of strength in being part of that crowd was amazing. Now *we* were the wood ants, except we had the power to think and do right. But the enemy was right alongside us and could strike at any moment. It soon became clear to me why the drums and chants were necessary. The alternative was panic.

There was no chance of looking for Amelie or Raff. We could see neither the front of the march nor the back and, in any case, moving through the crowd in either direction would only draw attention to us. As it was, the compers were paying no attention to us whatsoever, and if we were lucky it would stay that way all the way into Bluehaven.

We progressed maybe a few hundred meters, then, just as we were celebrating seeing the sign saying

WELCOME TO BLUEHAVEN, the march took a left turn into a smaller side road. No one was entirely sure what was going on, except that this wasn't the intended route. There was some discussion as to whether Comprot had agreed to the route in the first place, or whether the march, like most marches these days, was totally illegal— except it didn't look that way, not with the compers accompanying us.

I could sense the anxiety growing among the people around me. We were being funneled down a road with walls on both sides, hemming us in, leaving no escape route if anything kicked off. As if in response to this, or maybe because of the echoing walls, the chants and the drums welled up all the louder. Gradually, however, the march was slowing, and eventually we came to a dead stop.

It was only now we became aware of the commotion coming from the front of the march—angry cries, something which sounded like firecrackers and, in the midst of it all, a long, loud scream. Suddenly a girl appeared, not much older than me, fighting her way back through the crowd, imploring everyone to link arms and stand firm.

Now the adrenaline really started to pump. "What's

going on?" I asked.

"They've charged the front with horses," she gasped, as she made her way breathlessly back through the crowd.

We did as we were told and linked arms, all except for my one arm which held firm to Feela's basket. I could only imagine the panic that would be gripping her at this moment. She had hated Bonfire Night with a vengeance, and this was fifty times worse than that.

What I could not imagine was that was going on at the front of the march. All I knew was that people must have been acting with extreme bravery, because the horses hadn't broken through. If they did, it would cause a stampede, which could crush us all. For all I'd learned about Comprot and all those in power behind them, I still couldn't believe they would allow dozens, maybe hundreds, to die like this. Obviously I still had a lot to learn.

Suddenly there was a surge of people losing balance and falling backwards through the crowd. The surge was contained but it was enough to set some people off in a panic. One woman was yelling that she had kids with her, and the kids were crying hysterically. In response some guy offered them a leg-up over the wall, and as a result of this all discipline started to break down. People were giving legs-up all along the wall, breaking links and retreating, even pushing their way forward, armed with sticks and stones. Now the chaos was putting us into danger. If we didn't get crushed, it was odds-on we'd get arrested. After a quick and urgent discussion, we made the decision to take our chances on the other side of that wall.

Chapter Twenty-Six

It was as if we had moved into another dimension. On the other side of the wall was a cemetery, with neatly tended graves interspersed with attractive trees. There was no sign of Comprot, but the area was quickly filling up with small groups carrying flags and placards, most heading in what they must have guessed was the direction of the town center. We began to follow them, doing our best to stay close to the crowd. As we did so a small group of men appeared on the path ahead, heading towards us. Without warning, just as they reached the people at the front of the crowd—a teenage couple—one of the men punched the lad full in the face and laid him out cold. As his girlfriend yelled out in shock and anger, the men started laying into other demonstrators, who were at least forewarned, and fought back. It now became clear, however, that the men weren't alone. Figures started appearing all over the graveyard, some armed with sticks, a few with metal poles. Moments later the graveyard was a battlefield.

There was no time to make sense of this. All we knew was that this new enemy was vile, brain-dead and thirsting for blood. With Feela depending on us, we had no option but to get out of there as fast as we could. I ran for the cemetery gates, which were on the far right of the graveyard, but there were monsters there too and, to my horror, we were recognized by one of them. A deep, primitive howl went up among the enemy, and six or seven of them headed for us.

Was this all part of Comprot's plan? Was this how they wanted to deal with us, without having to bother about courts and lawyers and jail sentences?

Was this how I was going to die, in this tidy graveyard, under a blue sky, at the hands of idiots brainwashed just as I used to be?

One thing was for sure. I wasn't going without a fight. I hadn't come all this way to meekly surrender to a gang of grunting apes. And no one, but no one, was going to touch Feela. As the first loathsome individual grabbed me and forced his arm around my neck, I sank my nails into the flesh of his wrist and with every ounce of strength in my body brought down my teeth into his forearm. He gave a yell and a curse, and as I pulled out my teeth I cried at the top of my voice:

"Anyone else want it? Anyone else want cat flu?"

The first attacker released me. I found myself addressing a sea of ugly faces and saw very clearly, amongst all that gray-faced hatred, weakness. Fear. The same fear which had driven them to attack me was now preventing them carrying out that attack.

"You've heard of me, haven't you?" I yelled. "You know who I am! Well, come on then! You're not scared of a disease, are you?"

As the standoff continued, Kris came alongside me, picked up Feela's box and began coolly walking away—apart from his shaking hands, that is.

"Get the bitch," someone said. But no sooner had the words escaped him than he was crowned by a flagpole. Reinforcements had arrived over the cemetery wall. The odds had changed dramatically in our favor, and it was soon clear that the enemy wasn't as big and brave as they'd first made out. Some of them beat a hasty retreat while others were quickly circled by protesters. Someone yelled at me to get out now, and at the sound of approaching sirens, that's what I did. As I emerged from the cemetery gates Kris motioned me urgently across the road. He'd forced the gate of a school and was inside the playground with Feela. I raced after him and the two of us flew helter-skelter across a netball court and into the shadows of the building. Comprot had begun to arrive in force, pouring in endless red and black waves from their vans into the cemetery, just as hyped, no doubt, as everybody else.

It felt so wrong to be leaving our comrades to face that frightening force, them having just defended us from another enemy. But our escape was the aim of all this. If we went back into the open everything so far would have been in vain.

Kris was already focused on the school doors, but there was no way they were opening. We skirted around the side of the school and to our relief saw a window open a crack on the first floor. Without hesitation Kris shimmied up a drainpipe and, with his usual natural ease, clambered on to the window ledge, opened the window farther and snaked his arm inside to pull the catch. The window came open, Kris told me to get back to the doors, then disappeared inside.

Two minutes later, after some hectic searching for keys,

I was inside, beside a brightly painted mural saying WELCOME TO ADAMS GREEN SCHOOL— LEARNING TO SHARE, LEARNING TO CARE, beneath which was a visitors' book, which, in a strange moment of madness, I was tempted to sign.

We moved on down a corridor decorated in children's paintings of their favorite characters from books, a smiling photo of the pupils and staff, a commemorative plaque about the school's opening way back in 1954 beside a banner bearing a Viafara logo and the words WE'RE COLLECTING TOKENS FOR AFRICA. We decided to take the first door we came to, a green one labeled ACORNS—MRS. GROVER, since this classroom would give us a good vantage point over what was happening over at the cemetery gates.

It was a beautiful room, decorated with hanging snowflakes and mobiles, with wall friezes about cave art and where food comes from, writing and paintings by the children, a merit sticker board and a life-size papier-mâché-and-wire robot called Calculus. There was a small library of books and discs in one corner, and a random assortment of blue, green, red, and yellow desks around the room, some with stray workbooks and pencils still on them. On the far side, beneath the windows, was a table with a jar of paintbrushes and some pots of powder paint, one of which had been knocked over and spilled bright blue on to the floor, by some overeager hand at going-home time, no doubt.

For a moment I ached still to be sat at one of those colorful desks, in a safe, fair world—or at least a world that you could believe was safe and fair. But Kris was gesturing furiously for me to get to the window.

Out on the road a steady stream of protesters was being frogmarched out of the cemetery and lined up against the wall. Strangely enough, the people who'd started the fight with us were nowhere to be seen. Everyone else, however, was being treated like criminals: beaten if they showed any resistance, frisked, bags searched, belongings confiscated, then hauled off to the waiting prison vans.

Suddenly my eye was caught by something familiar. My jacket. They'd arrested the girl who'd swapped it with me and were frisking her. To my horror, they drew something out of her pocket and examined it with interest.

"Kris," I said. "That's the cat food you put in my pocket."

"Did I?" replied Kris.

"This morning," I said. "Don't you remember?"

Kris did remember. "Cool it," he said. "It's OK."

But it wasn't OK. The comper who'd found the cat food summoned his superior, they talked, then the superior got on his mobile. A minute or so later another van appeared, and out of this van came two dogs.

The girl was asked to take off my jacket, and the dogs were given the scent of it. Vaguely I remembered some statistic I'd once learned: A dog's sense of smell is a hundred times more powerful than ours. Those dogs would certainly smell me on that jacket, and probably Feela as well.

My worst fears were confirmed as the two dogs led their owners across the road directly to the playground gates, which the compers would soon see had been forced open.

There was no time to get out of the school now. Suddenly our sanctuary had become our trap. We grabbed Feela and hurried from the room, down the corridor, and up the nearest stairs. Kris had an idea we could maybe get on to the roof, while my mind was playing with some crazy idea that I could find a sink and wash off my scent.

There was no sign of a way on to the roof or into an attic. What we did see, however, was a school library, on the far side of which was a fire escape. With the sound of boots thundering across the playground, we had to make decisions quickly, and it seemed the best option. Luckily we found a key on the inside of the door and locked it. The mobile book cabinets at least gave us some cover, and the fire escape a way out. We crouched down behind the Action Books for Boys section, face to face with *Boy Comper, Terrorist Hunter* and *Axel Fortune: Rock and Roll Spy*.

Down below there was a crash. They'd forced the door.

Kris's eyes, however, were looking upwards. "That's a suspended ceiling," he said. "We can get up there."

In fear of my life, I accepted Kris's word. "Come on then," I said.

Kris leaped out of our hiding place and up onto a table. The ceiling was made up of acoustic tiles supported by a metal frame. Kris pushed at one of the tiles, and miraculously it moved. He flipped it upwards, leaving a square hole just large enough for us to squeeze through.

"You first," he said.

Kris offered me his two knitted hands. I placed Feela's box on the table and climbed up after it. With the aid of

Kris's leg-up, I got my hands inside the metal frame of the ceiling, and with strength I never knew I had, hauled myself into the narrow dark space above it.

Kris pushed Feela's box into the hole, and I made it secure. Then he leapt like a salmon, got both hands into the entrance, and with me pulling for all I was worth, scrambled up. We replaced the tile and recovered our breath.

At first I could see nothing. I opened the lid of Feela's box and stroked her head, to reassure her and, more importantly, myself. If we failed now it might be the last time I touched that warm fur.

Gradually, however, my eyes were adjusting. There was a tiny amount of light filtering through a small crack in one of the tiles. This also gave us a vague glimpse of what was happening below, which so far, thankfully, was nothing.

Kris adjusted his position and very nearly kicked me in the face. As my eyes adjusted a little more, I saw the sole of his shoe right before my eyes—and on that shoe a patch of luminous blue.

"Kris!" I whispered. "You walked in the paint!"

"What paint?" murmured Kris.

"There was paint spilled in the classroom!" I hissed.

"Didn't you see it?"

The reply was a splintering crash below us, followed immediately by an acrid smell of smoke. The view of the library through the cracked tile vanished, then flickers of laser-light lit the room. Men were down there now—it sounded like dozens of them. Footsteps rampaged around the room with the occasional loud shout, then, finally, the movement stopped. If we'd left a trail, obviously they hadn't seen it. Either the paint had worn out or the smoke had made them unable to see it.

The smoke was having another effect, however. From inside Feela's box came a small, pitiable cry. After all she'd been through, poor thing, now Feela's eyes were smarting and, possibly, her lungs. In a desperate attempt to keep her quiet, I reached into her box to comfort her. In my blindness, however, my hand caught her on the lower half of her belly, something she would not tolerate at any time, let alone when she was in distress. She mewled loudly and lashed out at me. Somehow I stifled a cry of pain, but our fate was already sealed, courtesy of a loud barking dog below.

A few seconds of agonizing suspense passed. Then, suddenly, a ceiling tile centimeters away from me burst away to reveal the handle of an automatic weapon. Then next time that handle pounded into the ceiling, it was right beneath my arm. This time I could not hold back the cry.

Laser-lights shot through the ceiling tiles. If those lights were followed by bullets, we would be blown to pieces.

"Get down now!" came a gruff yell. "One move and you're dead!"

The comper didn't exactly make sense, but we got his meaning. I lowered myself through the missing ceiling tile, was seized before my feet hit the desk, yanked brutally to the floor, and presented with a gun barrel to the head.

Kris followed, without Feela at first, only to be told, furiously, not to play games. Without protest, he lifted down Feela's box, which was immediately confiscated by the comper giving all the orders. As Kris reached the ground he was kicked full force in the stomach by another comper.

"That's for Joe," grunted the comper, as Kris sank to his knees.

The comper in charge said nothing, merely removed his helmet and instructed the others to do the same. He was a big man with blond hair and a world-weary expression.

"It's in here, is it?" he grunted, turning his attention to Feela's box.

"*She*," I replied.

The big man ignored me. He got down on his haunches, eye-level with the box, then slowly pried the lid open just a fraction, watching with extreme care, as if unlocking a safe. Once satisfied, he got on his mobile.

"We got 'em, sir," he said. "Yeah, both alive. And the cat."

The big man closed his phone and we all waited.

Chapter Twenty-Seven

It was three men who eventually walked into the room. One had the cap and insignia of a Comprot commanding officer. The other two wore white chemical suits, minus the headgear. One carried a briefcase. The other carried a plain white plastic box.

The officer stopped in front of Kris and looked him sharply up and down, like a robot programming itself with essential information. Then he did the same to me.

"You've caused a lot of trouble, young lady," he said, in a monotonous nasal voice.

"The cat's here, sir," said the big comper, with a hand on Feela's box as if it was his own personal prize.

The officer walked slowly over to the box, then looked around his men with a sarcastic half smile. "I'd call that animal cruelty, wouldn't you?" he said.

There was an obedient laugh.

"Thought they were animal lovers!" added the officer, clearly enjoying his little performance.

Another laugh.

The officer's manner changed. "OK, Dr. Stott," he said, in a firm, efficient tone. "Do the business."

The two white-suited men went to a nearby desk. The taller man placed the white box on the desk, while the other opened the briefcase and took out a number of small items, housed in plastic bags.

"Pentobarbitone?" asked the taller man, and the other indicated a bottle.

The taller man selected a second bottle, not the one indicated, then began assembling a hypodermic needle.

"No!" I screamed, but as I tried to leap towards Feela, at least two compers seized me.

"Bastards!" yelled Kris, but got another kick for his pains.

"Kill me! Kill me instead!" I screamed. Everything had gone unreal, out of time, beyond even nightmares.

Dr. Stott, if that was his name, worked with quiet efficiency, unmoved by my hysterical screams. He opened Feela's box, assessed the contents, and placed his arm decisively inside. That awful sound arose, the sound only made by Feela in submission. Though I could not see her, I knew exactly how she looked at that moment, ears and eyes flattened, dignity stolen, yet still with that impeccable beauty, and still, no doubt, awaiting the glimpse of a chance to make her sudden escape.

But this time there was to be no escape for Feela. Dr. Stott gave the needle a little squirt, brought it carefully down, found his mark, and emptied it. Then silence from the box, and all meaning drained from my universe. Winded and wounded, Kris cursed again, and took another beating.

The officer seemed to be enjoying my suffering. He let me sob for two, maybe three minutes, before advising me to shut up. "It's only sedated," he said.

"What?" I croaked.

"We haven't given it the lethal injection," said the officer.

"You haven't put her down?" I gasped.

"Not yet," replied the officer.

"What are you playing at?" I yelled.

"You have to understand we mean business," replied the officer.

"I don't understand *anything*!" I cried.

"The cat *will* die," said the officer, "unless you play ball."

"Play ball with *what*?" I yelled.

This officer was obviously a full-on drama queen. He gazed impassively at my frantic face, building the suspense, before speaking again in that measured monotone.

"You've been given an option," he said. "A very generous option."

The officer paused again, maybe waiting for me to look grateful.

"James Viafara has personally intervened," continued the officer.

This, needless to say, came from out of the blue. James Viafara was a well-known figure, even to people like me who couldn't name more than three businessmen. Most people simply knew him as the Cat King, since his company owned all the cats now that they'd taken over Chen, their only rivals. The Cat King was famous for his TV charity marathons and appearances on the popular reality show *Boom or Bust*. I couldn't say I'd ever had an opinion on him, though most people seemed to think he was OK—except Kris, of course. To Kris he was the devil made flesh.

"Mr. Viafara," continued the officer, "has offered to have your cat registered and for you to purchase it."

"Purchase it?" I repeated. "How much for?"

"Forty thousand euros," replied the officer.

"Forty thousand euros?" I repeated, aghast. "I haven't got *forty* euros!"

The officer sighed. "If you hadn't gone on this stupid adventure," he pronounced, "you would know that you actually have a very tidy sum of money coming to you."

"What?" I replied. "How?"

"Your father's life insurance," answered the officer. "It paid out on the death of your mother."

Now I really was dumbfounded. I'd known, of course, about that insurance policy, but how or why it would ever pay out had been pushed to the back of my mind entirely.

"How do you know about my dad's insurance?" I asked.

"Terrorism and Aliens Act," replied the officer. "We have access to all your personal information."

The memory of Mum flashed into my mind—her need for privacy and dignity, and how horrified she would be at such intrusion. Not that I felt any different.

"It really is a very generous offer by Mr. Viafara," added the officer.

"PR," grunted Kris, but I kept my eyes away from him. I could see, of course, how they wanted to use me. I'd become a cause for the Free Cats movement, a figurehead, and Comprot wanted the world to see me toe the line. But the price of refusing was Feela's life.

"Will I still be arrested?" I asked.

"If the cat becomes legal," replied the officer, "we will write off the whole affair."

"What about Kris?" I asked.

"Kris will have to answer a few questions at the station," replied the officer. "After that he will be free to go."

This didn't seem to square with the beating they'd been giving him, but I reasoned that if I did the deal with Viafara, they wouldn't dare do Kris any more harm.

"Well?" asked the officer.

My eyes fell on the bottle they called pentobarbitone. At the thought of that needle going into Feela again, reason didn't come into it.

"OK," I said quietly.

Chapter Twenty-Eight

This was the day I had expected to end in Ireland, a police cell, or a morgue. Instead I found myself in the entrance lobby of the six-star Imperial Hotel, gazing in awe at the wonderland of marble, glass, fully grown trees, and people who seemed to have walked straight off a Paris fashion runway. Apart from Special Operations leader Harry Sewell, that is, who still wore the active service uniform and scruffy mop of blond hair I'd first seen at the school. It was Harry's job to supervise me but also ensure I got everything I wanted.

Harry was keen to check in and move farther into the hotel as soon as possible. Outside, compers were thick on the ground and workmen were erecting a temporary fence around the building. The Imperial looked out over the seafront at Bluehaven and would be a certain target for protesters once they knew I was inside, scheduled to meet their arch-enemy as soon as his helicopter touched down on the roof.

I wanted so badly to communicate with those protesters. I wanted them to know how much I valued what they'd done for me, and that I still totally agreed that cats should wander the earth freely and be owned by whoever wanted them. But I'd started on this journey to save Feela's life, and my priority hadn't changed. All that had changed was that I had a six-figure sum in my bank account and an offer I couldn't refuse.

The arrangements at reception were completed. I was given a room key, a pet permit, and a welcome pack outlining all the pleasures I could experience at Bluehaven's premier hotel.

"Lunch?" asked Harry Sewell, leading me into the ground-floor restaurant.

"I'll just have a roll," I replied, feeling ill at ease in the plush surroundings, especially with everyone's eyes anxiously focused on me and the box I carried.

Sewell picked up a menu and offered it to me. "Don't be a martyr, love," he said. "You can have anything you want."

"I just want a roll," I replied.

"Vegetarian, are you?" asked Sewell, opening the menu himself.

"Fishetarian," I replied.

Sewell made no comment. His calculating, world-weary eyes scanned the menu. "Wild mushroom risotto," he said. "How about that?"

I couldn't deny that the smells around the restaurant were making me salivate. The truth was, I was starving. Was it really such an important principle not to eat the best food when it was offered me?

"What about Feela?" I asked.

"What, you want her to have something off the menu?" asked Sewell.

This had not occurred to me, but the moment the big man said it, the idea appealed a lot. Yes, it would be fine to have wild mushroom risotto if Feela had the salmon—so that's exactly what I requested.

"OK," said Sewell, not batting an eyelid.

"And I want a meal sent to Kris," I added.

Sewell wasn't so keen on this proposal. But after a long pause he agreed, ordered all the meals and one for himself, and sent for some junior officer to take Kris's meal to the station. I had no idea who this officer was, but it did occur to me he could have been the man firing bullets at us the night before. He didn't look much more than twenty and gave me a nice smile.

The hotel wasn't going to let Feela eat in the restaurant, that was clear, so the meals were ordered to be served in my room, which we then went to. The room was on the fourth floor (not so easy to escape from if I had a sudden change of mind) and was the most beautiful space I had ever seen, all done out in peach marble, with huge windows overlooking the sea, an old-fashioned wrought-iron bed, ornamental desk, couch, chairs, coffee table, a personal bar, and a screen the size of a wall. Alongside the main room was a mirrored, ensuite bathroom with toilet, sink, bidet, shower, and giant jacuzzi, fittings of gold, and towels as thick as doormats.

Sewell checked out the window locks and removed their keys and the remote for the screen. He did this in his usual matter-of-fact way, without explaining and, frankly, I was too tired to question it. All I wanted now was to eat, sleep, and then to sign the contract with Viafara as quickly, quietly, and invisibly as possible.

The meals duly arrived, except Sewell obviously hadn't told them the salmon was for the cat, as it came with side salad, potato wedges, and a little pot of tartar sauce. I'd checked Feela every two minutes since they'd released me in the school library, and could see she was slowly getting less groggy and was probably ready to eat. Nevertheless, she was a cowed and disturbed animal. I had to lift her out of her box, stroke and reassure her for a long time before she would sniff the food. Eventually, thankfully, she took a nibble, then slowly began to make her way through the rest of the meal—minus the side salad, potato wedges, and little pot of tartar sauce.

Sewell sat at the desk and ate his lunch while I perched on the edge of the bed above Feela. If this had been a movie we'd have begrudgingly started to like each other or something stupid like that. In reality I felt nothing but embarrassment in his company, watching him chewing his chicken leg in the same dour, mechanical way he did everything. It was all simple to Sewell, you could see that. People who broke the law were villains and it was his job to bring them in. Except in my case, that is. Obviously people in power could ignore the law when it suited them and when that happened, Sewell would ignore it too.

There was a knock at the door. Sewell checked the peephole, then opened it. In walked Dr. Stott, the vet, carrying the same black briefcase he had brought into the library.

"What's going on?" I asked, immediately putting down my plate.

"You have been told there'll be a blood test?" replied Dr. Stott.

"No!" I said, anxiously glancing down at Feela, innocently taking her final mouthfuls.

"Obviously we have to check the cat for HN51," replied Dr. Stott.

"She hasn't got it," I blurted.

"We have to test her for it," insisted Dr. Stott.

There was no point in arguing. At least the test would prove what rubbish the media had been talking—although the thought did cross my mind that they could rig the result. I trusted no one in authority now.

"OK," I said unenthusiastically.

Dr. Stott went about his business. Just as Feela had regained some confidence, here she was giving that awful passive yowl again as his professional hand grabbed her scruff firmly and took his blood sample. Hopefully that would be the last time he went near her.

"The mobile lab's arriving shortly," he said. "We'll have the result in a couple of hours."

I nodded, he left, and Sewell wiped his mouth. "I should get some sleep now, if I were you," he said.

"Not with you sitting there," I replied.

"You know the conditions," he said.

Sewell was referring to the agreement we'd reached in the library: I could hold on to Feela before the meeting with Viafara, but was never to be left alone with her.

"I'm not going anywhere, am I?" I pointed out.

Sewell stood up, rechecked the window, and had a look in the bathroom for good measure, just in case there were any secret exits in there.

"I'll be right outside the door," he said.

That was good enough for me. As the door closed behind Sewell I dropped on to the bed and loosed a sigh of relief, followed by a smile of familiar amusement as the tips of Feela's huge ears appeared over the edge of the mattress. For a moment I was back at home again, part of that everyday ritual which was unique to Feela. First the ear tips, then the pause of about five seconds, then the silent, weightless spring on to the bed. Sure enough, up she came, and to complete the ritual I pretended to be asleep. First she pushed her head against my hand then, when I didn't respond, she took her paw and tapped me gently twice, on the forearm this time. That, of course, was my signal to tickle her chin, which she duly stretched out to complete the pleasure.

Forget what had happened. Forget the traumas, the conflicts, and the pain. Feela was alive. I had kept my word to Mum—because if we hadn't tried to escape, we would never have become headline news, and James Viafara would never have made that offer.

I sat up and drew my finger down the back of Feela's head, where the black and ginger halves met in a perfect straight line, on down between her little shoulder blades and along the spine to her tail, giving her a gentle shiver. I remembered the time when Kris first showed his mastery over Feela by rubbing the base of that spine. Though I was about to sign the contract of ownership, I didn't want to deny that Feela was Kris's cat too. I wondered idly if we might live together—not like a couple, just friends . . .

. . . Yes, it was better to be friends. Friends liked each other, couples fought . . .

. . . On the other hand . . .

"What do *you* think, Feela?" I asked.

But Feela didn't think, I knew that. Feela was drawn to pleasure and repelled by pain. But what if something, or someone, gave you both?

I'd never been like the other girls in my class. If they fancied someone, really fancied them, they just lost all sense of perspective. I had too much of my mum's sensible streak for that.

On the other hand, Mum had always felt OK about Kris. She could see beyond his act, beyond his insecurities. If I went by her judgement . . .

Yes, that was it. I'd go by Mum's judgement. Then I could do what I wanted to do anyway.

I sank back on to the pillows, reliving those intimate moments at the waterfall, imagining some frightening but exciting moments to come. I wondered how long they'd keep him at the station, and whether he'd be here by the time I'd finished with James Viafara. If not, we'd arranged that Comprot would take me to the station to meet him, but I really didn't want that.

With my hand buried in Feela's warm fur, and memories and dreams of Kris merging into one, I drifted into a deep, peaceful, desperately welcome sleep.

Chapter Twenty-Nine

I woke up in total confusion, not knowing where I was, what time it was, what day it was even. But one thing was for sure. My moment of peace was over. Outside, in the gathering dusk, yells, chants, and drums signified that the news about Viafara was out. To add to the mayhem, someone was hammering on the door. I opened it to see Sewell, looking impatient and decidedly unfriendly.

"Get yourself together," he ordered. "The man's arrived."

Sewell waited, arms folded, as I put on my shoes and brushed my hair. His lame attempt to be friendly was over, and I could sense his hostility without even looking at him. I could tell he blamed me for the row outside and the pressure he was under, as if I'd personally invited the protesters, rather than wishing they'd simply forget about me.

"You'll be speaking to his personal assistant first," Sewell said, when I was ready. He led me to the lifts then down to the ground floor. As the lift doors opened I was hit by a barrage of noise and activity which my still bleary eyes could hardly take in. There were compers everywhere, some of them in urgent talks with black-suited hotel managers and gray-uniformed hotel security. There were people lugging bags and boxes of equipment through the lobby, and a bunch of cameramen who surged straight towards me, only to be told by Sewell in no uncertain terms to get away or get nicked. Through the glass doors of the entrance I caught a glimpse of men with dogs, the completed security fence, and beyond that the baying crowd. Sewell, however, was keen to get me away from the lobby as soon as possible, into a room called the Carlton Suite, which turned out to be empty except for a long, executive-style table and a woman who rose sharply from her chair to greet me. She was smiling, but the eyes which cased me up and down could not hide their disapproval.

"Hi-i!" she said, in a false-friendly voice. "I'm Livvy. You must be Jade."

The woman gave me a flimsy handshake. She was probably in her mid-twenties, blond, immaculately turned out from her ears to her fingernails, wearing a lilac tunic-suit over neatly tanned and toned limbs.

"We're just going to go through a few things, Jade," she said. "Would you like to take a seat?"

I sat. Livvy smiled. "That's the cat in there, is it?" she asked, eyes on the box beside me.

"Yes," I replied.

"Could I take a peek?" asked Livvy.

I opened the lid. Livvy glanced quickly inside. "Oh, she's lovely," she said. "I can see why you . . ."

Livvy trailed off and shot an anxious glance at Sewell, who had sat himself on the opposite side of the table.

"I won't touch him," said Livvy. "Not till we've had the vet's report."

"*Her*," I corrected, wondering who exactly had invited Livvy to touch Feela in the first place.

Livvy returned her attention to me. "Tell me, Jade," she said. "Have you had any media training?"

"Media training?" I repeated. "What's that?"

"You didn't do it at school?" asked Livvy.

I shook my head.

"It's important that you're prepared for the kind of questions you may get asked," said Livvy.

"Who by?" I asked.

"The media!" replied Livvy, baffled at my baffledness.

"I didn't know there was going to be media," I replied.

"Jade," announced Livvy, with a trace of concern, "this is a *media event*."

"I thought I was just signing a contract," I replied.

"Yes," replied Livvy, "but you didn't think Mr. Viafara was coming all this way without getting a news slot?"

"No one told me anything about the media," I said.

"Yes, but it's obvious, isn't it?" asked Livvy.

"Not to me," I replied.

Livvy looked a little impatient. "Well, just so you understand," she explained. "We have the event planned for the Ambassador Suite at seven PM, and in attendance will be all the major news, j-format and reality media, plus our legal people and invited guests. There's a strict guillotine on audience input at 7:50, but until that time you may be asked a number of questions. It's very much in your interests that you take our advice concerning these. Particularly as you haven't had any media training."

A wave of awful depression came over me. How had I managed to fool myself that there would be some small, discreet signing ceremony before I'd slip off into the night, back to a quiet, happy life? None of this was happening for my benefit. I was here to be used.

"If you like," added Livvy, "we can also give you the use of Mr. Viafara's stylist."

'No thanks,' I replied.

"He's very good," said Livvy.

"I'm happy how I am, thanks," I replied.

"Up to you," said Livvy. "But I will warn you, the screen puts four kilos on you."

Livvy awaited my reaction with a grave face, as if she had just told me a nuclear war had broken out. From that point I found it increasingly difficult to listen to her at all. As she ran through her lists of dos and don'ts for dealing with the media she became like a strange, talking doll, mouth opening and closing, practiced expressions coming and going, none of it having the slightest relevance to the grim battle of existence in which I was involved. I vaguely wondered how much they paid her for this.

Sewell, at least, was taking an interest. A couple of times I glanced over to see his world-weary eyes slowly scanning her up and down as if she was something he was about to choose from a canteen servery.

What a world, I thought. What a world to come back to. How wonderful Kris suddenly seemed.

It was a call to Sewell's mobile which finally put an end to Livvy's prattle. The results of Feela's blood test had come through. Livvy reminded me how lovely it was to meet me, then departed briskly to attend to Mr. Viafara. That left me alone again with Sewell, because we were to wait there till Stott arrived.

It was a long wait. Even though I was sure Feela was not ill, there was always that tiny seed of doubt, and my head was in such a mess now that this seed grew into a fully grown tree of terror. It didn't help hearing Sewell on his phone every few minutes, discussing the events at the front of the hotel, where things were clearly heating up. I wished so much Kris was with me, but of course I had no way of contacting him or knowing when he would show up.

At last the agony was over, or so it seemed. Stott walked in, accompanied by a man in plain clothes who nevertheless had Comprot written all over him. Before they had said a word to me, however, they took Sewell aside and had urgent murmurings with him. I couldn't make out a word but there were several glances at Feela's box, each one seeming more sinister.

"I need to have a look at the cat again," said Stott to me, finally. He opened the lid of the box, scrutinized Feela closely, then began feeling about her body, intense concentration on his face. When this was finally done to his satisfaction, he sat down.

"The good news is," he began, "your cat is not infected with HN51."

That certainly was good news, and the fact he said "your cat" was heartening too.

"However . . ." he began.

What now? A new disease? A fatal condition?

". . . the cat is pregnant."

Of course. Why had I not realized they would discover that? I had to think up some excuses fast.

"Pregnant?" I repeated, trying to sound surprised. But I'm no actress.

"You knew she was pregnant," said the plain-clothes man. He had a head of tight black curls which looked suspiciously like a perm, and what looked like a fake tan as well. Something about him reminded me of a shop-window dummy, except not as friendly.

"No I didn't," I replied.

"Your boyfriend told us," said Fake-Tan Man.

This threw me completely. Surely Kris wouldn't have

told them anything! On the other hand, what might they have done to him, or threatened him with?

"He's not my boyfriend," I replied lamely.

"How did she get pregnant?" pressed Fake-Tan Man.

"I don't know!" I lied. "It must have happened before I found her."

Stott shook his head. "This is a very recent pregnancy," he announced.

My tired head searched for a believable story. "I'm not always watching her," I blabbed. "She does go outside."

"Don't waste our time," snapped Fake-Tan Man. "All legal males are neutered. This cat's met with an illegal."

"No she—" I began.

"What we want to know," continued Fake-Tan Man, "is where and when."

I clammed up.

"Your boyfriend's already told us," added Fake-Tan Man.

"Then why are you asking me?" I asked.

"To check his story," replied Fake-Tan Man.

"What was his story?" I asked stupidly.

Fake-Tan Man gave a sarcastic smile, to let me know exactly how amusing he found this question. At this point there was a brief knock on the door and Livvy reappeared.

"Everything's ready to go," she said. "We need Jade in five minutes."

Fake-Tan Man nodded, Livvy left, and all attention was back on me. "You'll be going nowhere tonight until we get an answer," said Fake-Tan Man.

"I've been promised!" I cried.

Sewell held up a hand. "You've been promised to keep the cat," he pronounced. "That still applies."

"And to go free!" I cried.

"You'll go free as soon as we have the information we want," replied Sewell.

"No one said that!" I cried.

"You never told us the cat was pregnant," snapped Fake-Tan Man. They'd slipped into a good-cop, bad-cop routine.

Sewell checked his watch. "We've got to wrap this up, Conor," he said.

Fake-Tan Man gave an impatient sniff and pointed a finger in my face. "You listen to me, *love*," he snorted. "I've got no say in this deal, and I don't have to like it, but I'm going to make one thing clear. No one's going spreading a pandemic around this country on *my* watch.

Once this show's over you are coming with me and you are telling me everything you know about how this cat got pregnant. I've got the same message for you as I've got for that mob out there: Observe the law and you have nothing to fear. Break it, and I will break you."

There was something so sinister in the way Fake-Tan Man made everything so personal. I really felt I was in the presence of a playground bully, except this bully was paid by the government, and there was no one, absolutely no one, to run to if he victimized me.

"Come on, love," said Sewell, rising from his chair. "You can still be home tonight."

"No, no," replied Stott, correcting him. "Not tonight."

"Why's that?" asked Sewell.

"We can't do the operation till tomorrow," replied Stott.

"What operation?" asked Sewell.

"The hysterectomy," replied Stott.

The word hit me like a truck. One of Mum's friends had had a hysterectomy. They had cut her womb out.

"You're not touching her womb!" I said.

It was as if I'd said nothing. The three men discussed the practicalities of the operation to remove Feela's womb and abort her kittens as if I wasn't there. Once they'd sorted these details out and pronounced themselves satisfied, Sewell picked up Feela's box and asked me to follow him. I continued to argue, offering to have the kittens registered, pleading for them to let nature take its course. In the middle of this Livvy reappeared, looking almost panic-stricken.

"Mr. Viafara's waiting!" she cried.

"So?" I snapped.

Livvy stared at me with an expression of absolute bafflement. "Mr. Viafara is waiting!" she repeated.

"Let him wait," I replied.

Livvy's look of bafflement turned to one of outrage. Sewell stepped in aggressively. "Listen here, love," he growled at me. "You go out there now and do what you've agreed to do, or you will be spending the next thirty years behind bars."

"And your cat," added Fake-Tan Man, "will be in the incinerator."

My protests dried. With my head in turmoil and my body suddenly feeling hopelessly weak, I left the room behind Sewell and Feela, and walked shakily through the giant lobby of the hotel, hardly registering the continued mayhem outside the front doors. Up ahead were the doors to the Ambassador Suite, guarded by both

Comprot and hotel security, but we weren't entering the room that way. Livvy's heels went *clack-clack-clack* with total singleness of purpose around a maze of corridors until we reached the rear of the hotel and another entrance to the suite. Despite the state I was in, it had become second nature to me to map out my surroundings, check the exits, note the signs. I clocked a back entrance to the hotel, heavy with security cameras, turnstiles blocking the ways in and out, keypad lock on the door. I spotted toilets, an office, and a green room, presumably for performers in the Ambassador Suite. I noted that, compared to the front entrance, security was virtually absent here.

Livvy reached the door she was seeking and issued final instructions. Sewell was to take Feela in and put her in the prepared box. I was to follow Livvy to my seat, await my cue to shake hands with Viafara, authorize the payment from my insurers, sign the contract, and accept the Viafara collar which would then be fitted on Feela. Questions would follow which I should field as instructed. Any deviation on my part would mean the immediate termination of the event, the consequences of which were well understood.

My mouth dried. My heart thumped like a drum.

Livvy tapped a number into the keypad and opened the door to reveal a room packed to the brim with cameras, microphones, and hyped-up, staring people. Straight ahead of us was a stage area where James Viafara sat next to an empty blue leather and chrome chair in front of a screen with the Viafara logo and the words WORKING WITH NATURE FOR A SAFER FUTURE. In front of the chairs was a glass table on which sat a Viafara platinum-X collar, a transparent pet box with the Viafara logo, some papers, and a large ornamental ink bottle in which was an old-fashioned quill pen, the kind I'd seen in books about the Victorians.

Viafara turned to look at me. He seemed unnaturally clean, almost like a waxwork, in an impeccable silver jacket over a black polo-neck. He was, of course, a celebrity, a professional, who'd been in these kinds of situations a thousand times and knew exactly how to milk a crowd. They trusted him, just as I'd trusted him once. Now, however, I saw with crystal clearness that this man was my enemy. This man wanted to have my cat's womb removed and her kittens terminated. He wanted this so his firm could go on making profits and he could keep his private islands and jets and customized wardrobe.

"That's for you," urged Livvy, indicating the empty chair.

By now every eye was upon me. Flashguns popped and a hubbub of murmur filled the room. James Viafara's expression was becoming mildly exasperated.

"Will you please take your seat!" pressed Livvy.

It was an impossible situation. Now I was here, now it was really happening, I knew I could not go through with it. But neither could I sentence Feela to death.

"I need to go to the toilet," I said.

Livvy slapped her hand dramatically against her forehead, then marched into the arena and whispered in Viafara's ear. As she returned he shared a joke with the crowd which I missed but which they obviously found amusing.

"Please," she said. "Two minutes at the most."

Sewell immediately clamped himself to my side. Feela was left in Livvy's care as I was escorted like a death-row prisoner out of the room—leaving the door open—back down the corridor to the ladies' toilet. Sewell knocked on the toilet door, gave the place a quick once-over, then ushered me in—thankfully taking himself outside. I went straight to one of the cubicles, sat down, and fought to compose myself.

This was like no toilet I'd ever been in before. It even had a TV screen set in the door. Ha! I thought. Sewell missed that. For no reason other than bloody-minded disobedience, I pressed the on-pad.

At first I couldn't take in the newsreader's words. All I saw was Kris's face, a recent picture of Kris's face, with the words DELANEY ESCAPES CUSTODY—DELANEY ESCAPES CUSTODY running across the screen below it. When the shock of this had faded, fragments of the story began filtering through to me: Kris Delaney, arrested under Terrorism and Aliens Act, also charged with theft, assualt, abduction of Jade Jones, assaulting a community protection officer . . . being transferred from Comprot station to maximum security detention center . . . escape may have involved others . . . details unclear . . . public warned not to approach under any circumstances . . .

That was enough. Enough to know I'd been conned, enough to make up my mind, enough to send me charging from the toilet, past a startled Sewell, back through the open door into the Ambassador Suite. High on emotion, unafraid of anything, I marched center stage. The room fell utterly silent, and next moment I heard my own voice, loud and strong and inevitable, as if it was pre-recorded:

"I am not a criminal!" I cried. "I have stolen nothing!"

I turned to Viafara and pointed an accusatory finger. "This is the criminal!" I cried. "This is the thief!"

My eyes fell on the table prepared for my sacrifice. I seized the ornate ink bottle and with one decisive sweep of the arm sent the contents cascading over James Viafara.

"Victory to the Free Cats League!" I cried.

There was a moment's utter shock—not least from Viafara—then pandemonium. A surge of people came forward, cameras flashing, voices yelling and, in the midst of them, to my amazement, a Free Cats League banner. Punches were thrown between the people holding this and the security guards, and the next second Comprot had opened fire with electric stunners.

I had not lost my new talent for clear thinking in the most desperate situations. In the center of all this chaos I saw both Feela's box and my escape route. Sewell was fully occupied with a demonstrator and only Livvy barred the way. In seconds I had the box in one arm while the other dealt with Livvy—not a hard strike but perfectly timed, enough to dump her on her perfectly toned backside. As I escaped through the exit door I slammed it shut, knowing the keypad would delay my pursuers for the vital seconds I needed.

Luck was with me. As I reached the back entrance a man was coming in. I placed Feela's box beside the turnstiles, vaulted them all at once, grabbed the box again, and charged past the baffled incomer and out of the hotel.

Was I fated to escape? It was beginning to feel like that. Making that speech, standing up to one of the most powerful men in the world, had made me feel invincible. Even though the rear of the hotel was guarded by a wall at least four meters high, I was convinced an escape route would open up for me. Sure enough I found the pedestrian entrance to the hotel's underground car park which I took without a second thought, hammering down a set of steps into an alien world of concrete and luxury limos, their gleaming hoods as unnaturally clean as Viafara. Somewhere there was an exit for those cars— surely that would provide an escape for me.

Footsteps clattered down the steps behind me. No need to look behind: They couldn't catch me. My laser sharp eyes had already spotted the golden arrows marked EXIT painted on the floor of the car park. Despite the weight of Feela I ran like lightning around the corners, up the ramps, between the cars, until it appeared before me: a mesh gate and gatekeeper's booth, on which the word FREEDOM was burning in letters of fire, if only in my mind.

The fact that this gate was closed did not bother me in the slightest. I went straight into the same routine we'd used to get out of the car graveyard—except instead of using a stone I simply kicked the nearest car, setting off an ear-splitting siren and bringing the security guard hurrying towards where I'd been standing. I was already gone of course, taking a zigzag route to the exit gate, all concentration focused on the controls to that gate, wherever they were.

As it was, I didn't even need to find them. As I raced up the final ramp, I must have crossed an electric eye, because miraculously the gate began to lift of its own accord. Truly, truly, we were fated to escape!

It was only when I ducked under the gate, however, that I realized where I was. My sublime confidence vanished like smoke as I found myself penned like an animal behind the high metal fence they'd erected at the front of the hotel, security lights blazing in my eyes. Almost at once the crowd recognized me and let out a deafening caterwaul. Whether they were baying for my blood or howling encouragement I couldn't tell, but it little mattered, because I was trapped like a rat without hope of escape. Compers surged towards me on all sides. Fate had betrayed me.

In that strange timeless moment many things went through my head. My first glimpse of Feela. Mum's face, gray with death. Holding Kris. The needle in Stott's hand.

No! I could not let it be!

In that fractional moment before they seized me, I played the very last card available to me. In all probability it would bring a quick end to Feela's life— but it gave her a chance, however minuscule, of survival.

I flicked open the lid of Feela's box, dropped it to the ground, and screamed at her to run. My scream was instantly silenced by a gloved hand over my mouth. Seized and helpless, I watched Feela's terror at the mayhem all around her. A terrified animal will either run like fury or turn to stone, and Feela, to my horror, was cowering and motionless.

The compers, of course, were also afraid. Being people who obeyed orders and shared the world-view of their masters, they bought into the myths about free cats more than most people. Nor were they trained in how to arrest an animal. For a few moments, then, there was stalemate.

Then they released the dogs.

Never in all my worst nightmares had I imagined it could end like this. I had seen these dogs in action at the cemetery, seen the savage way their jaws could seize a protester's arm. If Feela did not move fast she would be torn to pieces.

Thank God, however, Feela did move, and like lightning. The barking of the dogs was like a trigger, setting off her deepest instinct to survive. She tore away along the front of the hotel, the dogs in frantic pursuit then, just as they seemed about to catch her, turned on a sixpence and set off back towards us. The cumbersome dogs skidded to a halt, turned, and took up the chase with even greater vigor. Feela desperately tried one escape route after another, all dead ends. Her speed was fantastic, the speed of a sudden, natural huntress, but I knew the dogs had greater stamina, and the longer the chase went on, the more likely they were to prevail. As she ran hopelessly to the closed glass door of the hotel, Feela was cornered. For half a second, one of the dogs got half a hold on her, then she was away again, slaloming brilliantly between them, racing towards the crowd, which by now was screaming for the dogs to be called off.

Now she really was trapped. No way forward but the fence. Dogs to the left, to the right, and behind.

So Feela went up.

Even with all my knowledge of Feela's genius, all my awareness of her strong, supple body, I could not believe the miracle I was witnessing. Feela had shot up a vertical wall of wire mesh at least three meters high. As she perched precariously on its summit, the dogs leaped impotently at the fence, their furious barks only completing their humiliation. Meanwhile the compers desperately checked down their line of command for instructions on what to do next.

The drama wasn't over. Feela had gotten up, but she didn't have the ability to get down. Comprot were armed with a whole array of lethal and disabling weapons which they could use on her. Their frantic discussions would soon result in a decision on whether to stun her or kill her, though if she dropped from that height, unconscious, it would surely come to the same thing.

It was at this moment that a new hero—or heroine, I should say—came on the scene. A girl with flowing blond hair and tartan trousers was climbing lithely up the other side of the fence. If it were possible for a person to be part human, part cat, this girl was it. Amid howls of encouragement from the other protesters, her strong fingers grabbed and hauled, grabbed and hauled, till she was within reach of Feela. Only firm, decisive action would work at this point, and the girl provided it impeccably. Feela was swept off her perch and stuffed securely into the girl's zip-up jacket. Down she went, not quite as surely as she climbed, dropping the last meter or so into the now exultant crowd. Finally, as I gazed in wonderment at this angel of deliverance, she looked directly at me, gave me a thumbs-up of fantastic certainty, then melted into the crowd.

By now, I suppose, I was suffering some kind of hysteria. Even so, as the furious compers dragged me away to custody, I had an uncanny conviction that the mysterious girl with the blond hair and feline grace was wearing Kris Delaney's face.

Chapter Thirty

When the judge handed me a ten-year sentence, my first emotion was one of relief. Under the new Terrorism and Aliens Act, I could have gotten twenty-five. I'd refused to plea-bargain by giving any information about the Free Cats League or how Feela got pregnant, so many people expected me to get the maximum. That I didn't was maybe down to my age, or possibly the public outcry over the new no-jury courts.

They then told me I was going to Cold Knap Juvenile Security Unit, and my relief turned to dread. Cold Knap was one of the prisons run by Globex Security, and its reputation was appalling. Seven inmates had committed suicide there in the past year alone, and there were rumors of punishment beatings, filthy conditions, and corruption from top to toe. Even though I was hardened by my experience awaiting trial in custody, and the idea of prison itself no longer scared me, Cold Knap was a bleak prospect.

When it came down to it, however, I was amazed how well I coped—at first. It really was a vile place, but life on the road had hardened me more than I realized. Not only that, but I got respect from the other inmates for what I'd done, and incredible support from people on the outside, people I'd never met who sent me letters of thanks and encouragement—all of them vetted by the guards, of course.

Once I'd survived the initial week or two, however, I sank into a depression deeper than I'd ever known. The full reality of Mum's death finally hit me, and I cried nonstop for days, my loneliness no longer buffered by the presence of Kris or my beloved cat. To make matters worse, I had heard nothing of either of them. With the guards reading every letter and listening in on every conversation with a visitor, that wasn't surprising. In my saner moments I was glad Kris wasn't risking either himself or Feela—if he had Feela—by trying to make contact with me. But in the small hours of the night, in my bare and homeless room, I cursed Kris for abandoning me, imagined all kinds of awful ends for

Feela, and began to plot ways in which I could painlessly end my misery. If only, I thought, Mum and I had been out that night Feela strayed into our garden. If only I'd never met her or taken her in, and carried on with my normal life—gone to college, had a career, accepted the world I lived in without complaint—and been content within those limits.

Even as I thought these things, however, they frightened me, even more than the prospect of Cold Knap had frightened me. To have lived without Feela was not to have lived at all. And to live in ignorance, the way I'd lived before I met Kris and we'd begun our desperate adventure—that was to be a human pet in the hands of the Viafara Corporation.

Even now they were determined to train me to their ways. Twice a week we had citizenship classes to teach us how to be responsible and obedient members of society. Funnily enough, it was these classes which began to pull me out of the hopeless dark pit I had fallen into. I hated them of course, but so did most of the other inmates, and together we formed a kind of rebellious bond, a fellow-ship, a family even. Some of those inmates, frankly, were badly messed-up and unpleasant people. But there were others, as I discovered, who were just as aware as me of the twisted nature of the world we lived in, who hated not only the citizenship classes but the crooks who had stolen our cats and everything else they could lay their thieving hands on.

Amongst the new friends I made was Chloe, who had responsibility for stocking the prison library. The warders trusted Chloe because she had a mild, inoffensive smile and never put a foot wrong. They'd made a big mistake, however. Beneath her obliging exterior, Chloe was the biggest rebel in Cold Knap. She put me on to all kinds of books, some of them hundreds of years old, which nevertheless spoke to me as if they'd been written yesterday. I read dozens of them, from *The World Turned Upside Down* to the poems of Blake, from *Gulliver's Travels* to *Ten Days That Shook the World*. I began to see myself not as a lonely and isolated individual, but as part of a tradition of revolt which stretched back centuries. I was not the first person to find themselves in prison for doing what was right, and knowing this gave me a new strength, the strength to carry on.

Another friend I made was Rowan. Rowan had been in Cold Knap for five years and knew everything there was to know about the place—in particular, which guards were up for a bribe. Rowan claimed to have lots of contacts in the outside world, people who could get anything and everything and smuggle it into the jail. When I told her about Kris and Feela, she listened with interest, even though she hated cats and wasn't much more fond of boys. Rowan said she'd pull some strings for me, but I didn't count any chickens. Most people in Cold Knap liked to brag and bullshit—it was part and parcel of being powerless.

Then, one day, as we sat in citizenship class, Rowan pressed a small disc into my palm beneath the table, giving me a quick wink as she did so. I pocketed the disc, and with heart thumping, returned to my cell to secretly examine it.

The disc was about five centimeters in diameter and as thick as a finger. Around the side was a glass aperture and on the other side basic play, stop, and rewind buttons. Although I had never seen one before, I was sure this was one of the new palm projectors everyone was talking about. They held about five minutes of silent DT-format visual, which could be displayed on any small, white space.

I wasn't short of white space in my cell—I had four walls of it. But I had to wait seven agonizing hours till lock-up and lights-out till I could dare to try out the projector. Building myself a little barricade with my desk, chair, and bedding, I set up a tiny secret cinema in the corner of the room.

I had to prepare myself before I pressed that on switch. I had no idea who this visual came from, what was on it, and what effect it might have on me. In some ways, despite all I'd been through, pressing the switch was the hardest thing I'd had to do. But press it I did, and sure enough a small blue square appeared on the wall, followed by the maker's logo, some warnings about copyright, and finally a fuzzy picture of a foreign city taken by a shaking hand. It was raining in this city, but full of life, people going about their business with energy and a smile. The picture jumped to a tank, its gun barrel being used as a climbing frame by cheering youths. Then another group of young people, carrying off a massive sign which I recognized as belonging to the Cityline Bank—except it obviously wasn't attached to the Cityline Bank anymore.

Into the picture came an out-of-focus hand, giving a slightly comical thumbs-up sign. Then, suddenly, like a punch in the guts, Kris's face appeared. He'd grown his hair again and also a wispy, bumfluff beard, which looked appalling. But that didn't matter. It was Kris, he was alive, and the reality of his life was such a shock to my system I almost had to stop the visual.

The next moment, however, was a different kind of shock, another one I was unprepared for. The camera pulled back to show Amelie next to Kris. He put his arm around her and they both grinned. Then, just to confuse matters even more, Raff appeared on the other side of Amelie, and also put his arm around her.

By now I really wasn't sure what I was watching. As I had no idea who'd sent the palm projector, I could have been seeing something posted on the freeweb, something maybe Kris had not wanted me to see. The fact that there was no sign of Feela was also ominous.

I began to prepare myself for the worst.

The picture changed. It was a sunny day now. Kris was in shot again, his face deadly serious. He beckoned to the camera, which followed him down what looked like a country lane, a hedge to one side, a ditch to the other.

Kris crossed over to the ditch. He said something to the cameraperson—which of course I couldn't hear—and the camera momentarily pointed down into the dank water at the bottom of the ditch. When it came up again, Kris had crossed the ditch and was heading through a gate into a field of waving yellow corn, glancing back with a frown which could either have been anxiety or the effect of the blinding sun.

Then Kris stopped. He looked down. The camera caught up with him and followed his eyeline, first going out of focus then zooming in on a black shape in the corn.

At first I thought it was a discarded piece of clothing— a jumper or a jacket. Then, suddenly, miraculously, two unmistakable eyes appeared above it, black-lined like an Egyptian pharaoh, profound as the sun.

Feela!

It was only now that I realized that the black shape was actually Feela's back. From that angle it was impossible to see her other colors, but as the camera moved around her, the warm orange and brilliant white appeared as well—healthy, undamaged, immaculate.

But the revelation was not over yet. As the camera moved right around to the opposite side, it became clear that Feela was not alone in her oasis in the corn. Four wriggling kittens fought for position at her belly, their tiny paws pumping her for her milk. My spirit soared as I witnessed their struggle for life, the life that I had made possible, the life I had refused to surrender to the soulless profiteers of the Viafara Corporation. Those kittens affirmed everything I had done and made any amount of suffering worthwhile. Those kittens were the continuation of Feela's short life into a boundless future. Those kittens were hope itself.

The camera tracked back up to Kris's face. He was smiling now, showing off those gruesome teeth which I had once found so repulsive, but now saw as a part of an ugly beauty I would not change for all the world.

But the visual was still not over. There was one more jump, to Kris again, this time standing in an alley, with a look on his face I'd never seen before—sheepish; shy, even. In his hands he held a sign on which was scrawled the letter *I*. As I pondered this mysterious symbol, however, he tossed the card away, to reveal another beneath, this one reading "WILL," though it wasn't that easy to read, due to the atrocious handwriting.

Now there was a pause as Kris seemed to fight to pluck up courage, before finally flinging the second card away, to reveal a third and, as it turned out, final card.

The card read, "WAIT 4 U."